BOURBON & BLOOD

By Garrard Hayes

Bourbon & Blood
By Garrard Hayes
Copyright 2013 Garrard Hayes
All rights reserved.
Book design by Cigarjuice Press
This is a work of fiction. All of the characters, organizations, and events portrayed in this novel are either products of the author's imagination or used fictitiously.

For my wife Sandy. You're an amazing, beautiful and strong woman. You've made our home a special place filled with pride, happiness and laughter. Thank you for supporting my dreams and for listening to my endless blathering about books, movies and TV. I love you with all of my heart.

I wish to personally thank the following people for their help in creating this book: My parents for always believing in me, my son Max for running the plot through his little brain during our Sunday morning swims, my beautiful daughter Devan, anything is possible if you put in the effort, Cheryl Hackert Chatterton for being my first reader, Sherry, David & Isabelle Vaders, Jason Broad, Paul Colby, Joe Calviello, Peter Mello and Jonathan Giannetti for their encouragement and Francine LaSala my editor for her mentoring and professional insight.

PROLOGUE

I parked the Lincoln on 71st and walked up Broadway, then turned right onto 72nd Street. My boots pounding the gray pavement, the cement sidewalks sparkled with flecks of minerals that reflected off the streetlights, adding to the sensation that this night would be magical.

The busy city streets buzzed with energy, with couples. Watching them interact, holding on to each other, I longed to gaze upon her beautiful face, touch her silky hair, feel her soft lips pressed against mine, breathe in the scent of her perfume.

When I arrived at her building she buzzed me right in without checking to make sure it was me. This was a tough city, where anything could happen at any time, and I made a note to myself to tell her to be more cautious.

I ran up the stairs to her apartment and knocked

on the door. I heard heavy footsteps approach, but no one opened the door. After a few seconds I tried the doorknob. Surprised that it wasn't locked, I swung it opened and stepped in.

Just then, I felt something hit me hard in the back of head. A white flash of pain exploded in my brain, blinding me, and then darkness engulfed me in a deep black river of unconsciousness.

At some point later, I came to, slowly opening my eyes as a throbbing pain shot through my head. I couldn't see anything, but I could feel movement, like I was somehow now in the back of a van or truck. I squeezed my eyes shut and tried to channel my pain into anger. As I struggled to lift myself up, another sharp pain exploded at the back of my head and I dropped back to the floor as the vehicle raced to an unknown destination, each bump causing me great agony.

I realized why I couldn't see. My head was covered in what felt like a burlap sack, reeking of sour vomit. I tried to move my arms, but they were pinned behind my back.

Another jolt of pain shot through the base of my

skull. I blinked the pain away, but it was only temporary; it came right back and intensified until all I could feel was nausea. Then I blacked out in a swirl of gray and black shadows.

I became conscious again just as the vehicle screeched to a sudden halt. Two sets of strong hands roughly carried me out of the van, dragging my tied feet along the pavement for what felt like two hundred feet or more. They dropped me on the ground, and I grunted loudly from the impact. It knocked the wind out of me, and replaced the oxygen in my lungs with a dirty musty odor that made me cough. Then I blacked out again.

Coming to this time, I found myself strapped to a chair, my arms and legs immobilized, but at least now I could breathe freely without the stench of the sour-smelling bag that had covered my face. I tried to see where I was but all was dark except for one light bulb hanging over my seat. The back of my eyeballs throbbed with pain, while the ache in my skull made me nauseated again. I couldn't see beyond the lighted area of my confinement.

Having no focus or sense of time, it could've been

a few minutes or a few hours later when I heard the sound of heavy heels, thumping louder as they got closer. A door opened behind me then slammed shut, the sound echoing through the room and right through my aching head. The source of the footsteps walked around the edge of the darkness. I couldn't make out a face, just a deep male voice that growled, "You have a sweet, beautiful girlfriend. Don't you think it would be a shame if something happened to her?"

CHAPTER ONE

I never really liked drinking bourbon, but it does take the edge off. Drugs have never been my thing. I've smoked my share of weed and snorted mounds of coke, but drugs didn't make me feel any better in the end. Weed made me feel stupid, like my brain was slowly being sucked out through my ears. Coke made me neurotic, like a caged squirrel. The other bad thing about coke was, the only thing I wanted to do while partying was more coke. So bourbon was my drug of choice, though the down side to the drinking was that it left me angry and depressed. The only thing that made embracing my drinking problem any better was waking up to strong coffee the next morning.

I stubbed out my cigarette in a full ashtray and reached for a partially filled glass of Knob Creek on the coffee table. Taking a big swig, I immediately got the burn on my tongue. My chest heated up as the bourbon slowly slid down to my stomach. The bottle now empty, and my mood improved, I floated into a numb sleep.

At some point later, my eyes opened. My jaw was hanging wide open and my mouth was dry. Groggy, I got up off the couch, trying to shake off the sleep. Glancing at the clock on the wall, I saw it was already time to go meet my cousin Jimmy, who was waiting for me at the local dive bar, no doubt chomping at the bit to tell me the latest about his "work."

Jimmy does all the talking, and I do all the listening. We've always been like brothers and he's the closest thing to a friend I've ever had. Jimmy worked for a group of Irish thugs who took advantage of poor people on Manhattan's West Side. He wanted me to work with him, but I didn't want to hang out with his criminal associates.

I staggered out of my rundown one-bedroom apartment, closed the heavy metal door, and locked the three deadbolts. The stench of garbage and eye-burning curry in the hallway were both reminders that I needed a career, money, and better accommodations than this dump on 39th and Tenth. The problem was, I hadn't been able to get any kind of respectable work for over a year. Being in the Army for five years, you build up a nice stash of cash and there really isn't anything to eat up your pay. You can't buy a car, go out to fancy restaurants, or spend money on a pretty girlfriend. So I had some pay left, but it was running low. I needed to get some work soon.

I probably should've reenlisted in the Army but my tour in Afghanistan left me depressed and filled with horrific memories that stuck in my mind and invaded my dreams. Sickening images of war, children's faces streaked with blood and tears, the vacant eyes of the dead. I tried to forget, but most days the memories hovered over me like a cloud of sadness.

The vital things I gained from the experience were training in gunnery and explosives. Marksmanship and long range targeting became easier after days and weeks on the shooting range. We practiced speed shooting on small moving metal targets at all distances. I had also excelled at hand-to-hand combat using mixed martial arts. We were taught Combatives, which is a military form of Brazilian jujitsu for submissions and fighting in close quarters. I could be on my back losing a fight, pinned to the ground and sweep an opponent's leg, spin around, get their back and choke them out or break a limb. Aikido and Judo were also used for different situations, in which multiple attackers or an individual attacker's own force and body weight could be used against them. This was my favorite technique for disabling or throwing an adversary where lethal force was essential. Some were extremely effective in closed quarters, where a few precious seconds made the difference between life and death.

In one of my more successful sorties, I led a platoon of brave men into a war zone. We killed several enemy guards, rescued four of our captured soldiers, and returned them to the base. A medal would've been nice, but I was just as happy to make it out and bring our men home alive. I had managed to work my way up from Private to Sergeant after a series of these successful missions.

I finished my tour and returned to my old Hell's Kitchen neighborhood. No parade, no commendation, and not much family left.

My parents died in a tragic car crash when I was eleven and my aunts, my mom's sisters, raised me in an apartment they shared on 37th and Ninth. I was already old enough to have my own personality by then, but they did their best to keep me out of trouble and teach me to be a good person. I still try to remember my parents, but the trauma of losing them has blocked most of my earlier memories.

Staying out of trouble wasn't easy though, especially because Jimmy and me lived in the same house. He was about my age and was always getting caught for stealing or punished for talking back. The one good thing, we were as tight as brothers, always looking out for each other, during good times and bad.

Jimmy never left the area and probably never would. He was tall, thin, and had a ruddy complexion from drinking. His hair was long, dark, and greasy, and always seemed to be hanging in his face. His fingers were stained from nicotine, a side effect of chain-smoking. His nostrils were usually red and irritated due to his cocaine addiction.

Since we were kids Jimmy has always been entertaining, full of big stories, and always able to find amusement in other people's misery. I didn't have to say much when I was with him. Just sat, sipped bourbon, and listened. Some of his crazy stories were funny, but most were tragic.

Jimmy most liked to ramble on about his adventures collecting rent and loan money for his boss, and last night, when I'd met him at Healy's Pub, was no exception. Once Jimmy had a few drinks, he was primed to sing praise for his employer. Frank Sullivan was the big boss of a growing criminal organization, and a rising star in New York City's crime underbelly. Sullivan owned a few apartment buildings and made big money lending to unlucky immigrants. That's where Jimmy came into the picture.

Jimmy always had cash, an amazing feat with all his snorting and drinking, but he was well paid. He bugged me relentlessly to work with him, but making money off people down on their luck didn't appeal to me.

He pulled out a money roll and waved it a few inches from my face. "Look at this, Bill. All I have to do is go uptown, knock on doors, and collect rent. Oh, and sometimes I get interest."

He went on to tell me how he handled a stubborn borrower by smashing the guy's hand in a kitchen drawer. News in that building spread from the laundry room to the elevators to the front stoop. Since then, folks paid quickly, not wanting to have their fingers broken.

We went outside to have a smoke and get some air. Jimmy smokes harder than anyone I'd ever seen. He sucks on his cigarette with such passion you can see his skull and cheekbones with each drag.

He lit up, then blew the smoke over my head. "It's so easy," he said. "Come on, brother. You gotta join me on the next run." He paused to suck down his cigarette in what seemed like one drag. "When they can't make rent, they end up borrowing money and never finish paying."

Jimmy pulled out another cig, and lit it with the burning filter of the last. Smoke came blasting out of his nostrils, and kind of reminded me of an angry bull from an old cartoon.

"It's fucking brilliant!" he said.

Criminals who liked to prey on the poor and needy. This was far more depressing than my own situation.

"You don't see anything wrong with all this?" I

asked Jimmy.

He took a long drag of his cig, blew smoke to the side, and gave me a playful smile.

"Are you kidding, brother?" he replied, and chuckled. He lit up yet another cig from the filter embers of his previous one. He finished that one and we headed back inside.

Healy's was not the kind of place I'd look to find my next love interest, but I was ready for one. She'd be a beauty with eyes clear and bright, an attractive face with sharp features, silky hair, and a body to die for. She would be smart, kind, and witty. Except the kind of girl I wanted would probably be out with the girls at some swanky nightspot looking to meet an upwardly mobile young executive. She wouldn't be looking for someone like me. I had no job, no money, no prospects, and continued to hang out at Healy's with its dark, unfriendly atmosphere and toothless hardcore drinkers.

When I got back home I flipped on the TV, but at that time of night they show mostly crap--late night infomercials and news. I made one round through the channels and found an old episode of *Star Trek*.

Captain Kirk, such a big ham with his over acting and shoulder rolls. I kept it on, feeling my eyes become heavy. After a while I blinked awake to find I missed the end of the episode. I shut off the TV and crawled into bed. Sleep engulfed me immediately, like a thick blanket.

CHAPTER TWO

Sunrise lit up my room and I dragged myself out of bed. I grabbed a book from the bed table and headed into the kitchen. I made some coffee and sat on the couch to read.

I read a lot of books. It's better than TV and movies. Mostly, I like crime fiction and horror. I was on the last chapter of *Falling Glass* by Adrian McKinty. In it, an Irish tough guy hired by a corrupt businessman helps a woman in trouble and tries to unravel some ghosts from the past. I dreamed of taking a trip to Ireland as I read, and visiting a small town. Of seeing the countryside and hiking through green fields, hilly and peaceful.

Once I finished, the book and the coffee, I moved off the couch and got ready to go out. I put on my black jeans, a white button-down shirt, and black steel-toe boots. I decided to get out and take a walk, see the city up close. I loved walking among the buildings, hearing the street sounds, and watching the city girls, especially in the summer. I was hoping the walk might just inspire me to have a drink somewhere other than Healy's. Maybe some place where I could meet a nice girl.

Outside, the stifling heat hit me hard. Humid, thick, and oppressive. A warm breeze blew softly from the west, briefly bringing relief from the sweltering summer heat. Clouds, dark and dreary, were moving fast across the sky. I hoped it would clear up quickly as getting soaked on my stroll would only have added to my misery.

I started walking towards Bryant Park, the sounds of cars, taxi horns, and people talking filling my ears. I caught small bits of conversations as I passed groups of people, like flipping through TV channels and only hearing a piece of each show. I quickened my pace. The movement and rhythm felt good and cleared my head. As I passed the subway entrance on 41st Street, the stench of urine hit me and I let out a breath and a grunt of disgust.

I stopped at the park, thinking I might be able to strike up a chat with a beautiful girl on her lunch break, but it was kind of empty. Still too early for the business lunch crowd.

I took a seat on a bench, facing the back of the New York Public Library. A beautiful building, even from behind. I lit up a cig, leaned back, and relaxed.

The staff at the Bryant Park Grill buzzed around preparing for the lunch crowd, setting tables and fortifying their stations. Just then, I noticed three businesswomen walking in my direction. Drinks in hand, chatting and laughing as they came my way, I thought they might be fun to talk to.

"Good afternoon, ladies," I said with a smile as they passed me. "Sure is a beautiful day."

One smiled back, but said nothing, then looked away, embarrassed as they walked on.

I turned to see a waitress at the grill watching me, a smirk on her face. She was absolutely gorgeous, with blond-streaked hair pulled back into a ponytail and beautiful green eyes. It was like I got hit with a bolt of lightning. I couldn't take my eyes off her. She reminded me a little of that actress in The Rum Diary with Johnny Depp.

She put her hands on her hips and squinted at me. "No luck, huh stud?"

I smiled and adverted my eyes to my boots, a little embarrassed. I looked up. "Just trying to make friends."

She continued putting her station together, then glanced back to me. "That's not a very New York thing to do."

I recognized a southern accent, sweet and real sassy. "Are you from around here?" I asked.

She stopped her work and edged closer to me. "No sir. Born and raised in Lumberton, Texas." She said it with pride, like it was something special to her.

"I guess it's a special place," I said. "I've never been to Texas but I hear it's supposed to be real hot, with big stretches of flat farmland." People started to enter the restaurant's patio area. She watched them get seated, then turned back to me. "It's special enough if you have family that you love living there. Things are fixing to get busy here," she said, walking away. "Nice talking to you."

I laughed to myself. "Fixing?" I blurted. I'd never heard anyone use the term "fixing" that way before. It was unique and refreshing. I was amused.

"What's your name?" I asked.

"Dana. What's yours?"

"I'm Bill. Maybe I'll come by to see you again."

"You do that," she said, smiling.

I sat there for a while and watched her work. Her face lit up with excitement every time a customer came in. She focused on each person as she diligently took their orders.

At some point later, I headed back home. As I walked, the smell of street food reminded me I hadn't eaten, so I bought a Mediterranean chicken shish-kabob on pita from a Halal street vendor.

Walking west past a group of brownstone buildings, I tried to find a good place to eat and settled on one of the stoops. An old homeless man was going through the garbage a few stoops down. He looked in his late sixties, with a white beard, dirty clothes, and a shopping cart. He reached into the garbage, pulled out a couple of empty soda cans, and put them in his cart, along with what probably were all his belongings, packed up dark green plastic bags. Watching him made me feel too ashamed to eat, so I wrapped up my lunch and headed over to him.

"Would you like some chicken?" I asked.

"Sure. Thanks," he said, and I handed him my lunch.

"Excuse me, sir, what's your name?" I asked.

"Ronald Warkowski. Friends call me Ronnie."

"Can I ask you something? Did you serve?"

"I did. Army, 1st Infantry. Vietnam. You?"

I nodded. "Did folks treat you alright when you came back?"

"Yeah," he said, with an ironic laugh. "No, they treated me like I was some kind of freak and I didn't belong here. I thought about going back to the Army, but my guardian angels told me not to. I ran out of money, it didn't last. Then I couldn't keep a job for more than a few weeks at a time."

"You still get flashbacks?"

"Yeah, when I drink or party too much."

"How long you been on the street?"

"A long, long time son."

"You ever get help from the shelters?"

"Yeah, but I always get in trouble when I'm there. I have a little anger management problem. I don't like when people try to take my things. I've worked hard to hold onto this stuff and they're always testing me."

"It must be hard to keep your stuff out on the street with no way to lock your door."

"There's always some tough guy who wants to look through my stuff. Nobody touches my stuff. They think cause I'm old and dirty I ain't gonna do anything. I beat those mother's down every time. I don't take shit from anyone, especially some dirt bag thieves who try to..." he trailed off and looked around.

"Try to what, Ronnie?" I asked

"Shhh... They're watching us."

"Who's watching?"

"The government. They're always watching and listening in on me. I know too much, gotta keep moving or they'll find me."

I felt bad for the guy. He didn't come back the same from his tour. I'd seen it so many times before. "Hey, if you ever need a place to stay take a shower, come to my place. Here's my number and address."

I wrote the information on a piece of paper I

found in my wallet and gave it to him. I didn't expect to ever hear from him, but I wanted to do something.

He studied the writing for several seconds. "I'll let you know what I find out. He said, looking up and down the street to see if anyone was watching.

"About what?"

"Your place, but don't worry, I'll keep an eye on everything."

I reached into my pocket and pulled out a wad of singles and a five--eighteen dollars. I gave him the money. "Maybe this will help," I said.

"Bless you, son," he replied, staring down at the money in his hand.

Halfway back up the block, I stopped walking and turned around. Ronnie was now sitting on the stoop, eating and smiling.

At least one of us would have a good day.

Digging through my wallet, I found a ten buried between some receipts and headed to Ray's for a couple of slices. I sat by the window and ate like an animal, barely chewing my food. When I finished up the pizza I headed back to the apartment.

Back home, I crashed for a while. When I opened

my eyes again it was dark. The clock read ten thirty. Trying to shake off the sleep, I changed, took a quick look in the mirror, and headed over to Healy's.

Donnie was working behind the bar. A nice guy in his early forties, he was thin with a full beard and a shaved head. I guess he shaved his head because he was going bald. It was a good look for him.

"What can I get you?" Donnie asked.

I took a quick survey of the bar. The same old hard-drinking crowd, and of course no girls.

"Ever get any attractive women in this place?" I asked Donnie.

He stopped cleaning a beer mug. "Not a chance with this crowd."

A couple of greasy old regulars sat to my right, laughing loudly. I needed a new hang out.

"Black and Tan and a shot of Knob Creek, please."

The bourbon was strong and burned all the way down, warming my chest. The heat and flavor lingered on my breath. I chased it down with the other half of my beer, nice and cold. I wiped the foam from my lips.

"Double me up?"

"Sure, be right back."

I sat there drinking for a while, my edginess melted away and I became one with the stool and the bar. I didn't want Jimmy to show up and drag me off somewhere, so I left Donnie two twenties and headed outside. The air felt cool on my face and suddenly I felt more buzzed. I decided a walk would help sober me up.

The road was wet and shiny. The glare from streetlights and passing cars reflected off the wet pavement, mesmerizing me as the misty rain woke me up.

Recently someone had told me about a bar over by the West Side Highway. I figured it must be for bikers and never bothered with it, but for some reason, it seemed like a good idea to go check it out. It was called Hogs and Heifers Saloon and it looked like a dump, but it was packed. People were standing out front, laughing and smoking. I moved inside, and wove my way through the crowd to the bar. I was surprised to see girl bartenders.

Now that's more like it.

The atmosphere was dark and musty. Bras hung

from the walls and ceiling. A slight stench from the bathrooms offended my nose so I moved to the other side of the bar. A jukebox played loud heavy metal music, I think it was a Rob Zombie song, but the crowd was just as loud as the music.

I finally made my way to the far side of the bar to find a cute bartender working hard. She had straight red hair, rosy cheeks, and a big smile. She wasn't as cute as the waitress at Bryant Park, but she was attractive and I watched her for a while. Finally she came over. "What can I get you?"

"A Black and Tan would be great."

"The Tan is kind of flat," she shouted.

"Then I'll just have some Black."

"You got it."

She came back with a cold Guinness, and I gave her a ten. "Keep it," I said, with a slight smile.

She gave me a little smile back. No way was she from this city. I drank the Guinness, and people-watched but soon the noise started to get under my skin.

I wondered how many times a night these cute bartenders got hit on. The owner was smart to hire girls from out of town. New York girls have too much attitude to be friendly. Guys probably fall in love every night, drink too much, and over tip. I watched as guy after guy gave it a go, trying to be clever. The music was too loud for her to hear what they were saying, but she would get close each time, smile and nod.

Becoming frustrated, I let out a big sigh and maneuvered my way through the crowd. I pushed my way outside, the music thumping in my ears. The fresh air, if you could call New York City air fresh, was a welcome relief. I leaned against the wall of the bar for a smoke while I waited for a cab to pass, but it didn't look like there were going to be any so I started walking uptown.

The streets were desolate and quiet. Not much going on around the meatpacking district at three in the morning. Cars sped by as I continued walking east towards Ninth Avenue. Up ahead I saw someone coming up the block towards me. I moved to the left to let him pass.

"Hey bud, you got a light?" he asked.

"Sure," I said, a little buzzed from the beer.

I looked down and dug into my pocket. I took out

my lighter.

"Give me your fucking wallet!" he snapped.

A nearby streetlight reflected off his knife. I stepped back, my hands up.

"Okay, take it easy. I don't want any trouble."

Then in a flash, I grabbed his forearm, twisting it into an arm bar, and slammed him into the wall. A loud crack echoed on the quiet street. He groaned as all the air left his lungs. The knife dropped to the pavement making a clinking sound. Blood ran from his nose and mouth. Lowering him to the ground I realized he was out cold but still breathing.

I looked around to see if anyone was around before leaving him there. "I'll give you a light next time pal," I said.

I picked up his knife with my hand tucked into my sleeve and threw it into the drain. I didn't want him bothering anyone else when he woke up.

CHAPTER THREE

The next morning, I made coffee and was reading a new crime fiction novel when my cell phone started buzzing. Seeing Jimmy's name on the caller I.D., I ignored it. Yes, I desperately needed the work, but didn't want to join Mr. Sullivan's group of thugs. The buzzing stopped, and then a few seconds later it started up again. Figuring he wasn't going to give up until he got me, this time I answered. "You're up early. Special day?"

I heard him sigh into the phone, then take a big drag on a cig before he spoke. "What the fuck are you doing, Bill? I got a job for you, stop being such a fucking pussy."

"Stop hounding me Jimmy or I'll do a fucking job on you!" I snapped.

He backed off. "Okay, Bill sorry, I'm just trying to help you. It's just that I told Mr. Sullivan you didn't take any shit and kept yourself alive in a tough place."

I didn't want to think about my war days and I didn't want anyone else thinking about them either. "You promised not to tell anyone what I went through."

"I know, I know. But ignoring this ground-floor opportunity is insane. I stuck my neck out for you. Now that he wants to meet you, there's no taking it back."

"Jimmy, you know what?" I asked.

"Can I come by and get you now?" He asked cutting me off.

"I won't be home. I'm heading out to find my future love."

I hung up before he had a chance to reply. I grabbed my keys and left. My cell phone started to vibrate like crazy, a half dozen text messages came roaring in. Jimmy was relentless. I didn't look at the messages. He'd only just draw me in. Jimmy meant well, but I had to be smart. A wrong move with this bunch and my life would completely go down the drain. Anyway, he'd likely track me down. Jimmy had a real knack for finding things and people.

As I walked out of the building I took a deep breath of city air. Lighting a Marlboro Red, I took a deep drag and blew out the smoke. The first drag smelled of burnt paper and tobacco.

It was a beautiful day, much cooler, dry, and bright. I started walking west, weaving through the crowds on Broadway, tourists looking up at the skyscrapers and business people trying to get around them and get to work. I was headed up to 40th when a navy Crown Victoria screeched to the curb and someone pushed open the door.

Was I being arrested? No. It was just Jimmy and a friend. He spat on the road. "Get the fuck in Bill. It's time to go."

"Can't make out what you're saying," I said, trying to avoid him.

I leaned into the car to see who was driving. It was Kenny Shea, a nasty, heartless goon who I knew growing up. He had quite a reputation for being mean and tricky.

This should be interesting, I thought to myself.

I didn't want to go anywhere with Kenny, but he had different ideas about me.

"We got work for you," Kenny said. "We're going to make you one of the boys."

I looked around. "Can't you boys find anyone to join your club?"

"Ask your fucking questions later," he countered. "I don't care if you're conscious when you get there."

I got the threat and I slid into the back seat.

"Okay, where we going?" I asked. Neither Kenny nor Jimmy answered as Kenny peeled into the street and started driving.

Kenny Shea had made his name through brawling, stealing, and murdering. I always tried to avoid him. Having a dad in the FBI made him a slippery guy to pin a charge on. Even when arrested, his jail time was short and whatever damage he did was repaired through his old man's connections.

The violence that emanated from Kenny engulfed anyone in his presence. He could smack or rob someone as simply as drinking a glass of water. One time in high school, he was hanging out on the street when a young couple in their twenties walked by, holding hands. Kenny got in the guy's face and demanded his wallet. When the guy refused, he hit him with a wild right hook and knocked him out cold. He then rummaged through the unconscious guy's pockets while his date begged for help, holding her boyfriend's head. People walked by, but people knew Kenny. No one wanted to get involved. He showed the cash to his crew like a trophy, sneering all the while.

Kenny was not tall, but he was wide and solid. His brown hair in a crew cut, he had a stubbly goatee and wore a navy blazer, white button down shirt, and gray pants with a dark gray newsboy cap, which made him look more like a college professor than a hood--a good disguise for his marks. His condescending sneer was the closest he'd ever come to a smile.

On the drive I considered the danger of getting involved with these people. Of course, once I started, they would never let me leave. My employment would only end in jail or death. Yet here I was with them.

We pulled in front of McKenzie's Quality Dining, Inc., the main base of operations for all of Sullivan's ruthless crews. Located in the heart of Hell's Kitchen, a few blocks downtown from the Port Authority, it had easy access to mass transit, taxis, and the tunnel for a quick "out" of the city. From the front it looked like a nice place to take your girl to lunch or dinner, but if you had any sense, the second you walked inside you'd know something wasn't right. It was a social club for a group of Irish gangsters. The place was filled with rough-looking men dressed in blazers, sitting at small tables, having quiet chats. When I entered, conversations stopped and all eyes turned to see who had just walked in. It was unsettling.

I was led past a long cherry wood bar. Behind the bar was a large mirror fronted by rows of top-shelf alcohol. Mr. Sullivan sat at a table in the back. He was in his early sixties and slightly overweight with a clean-shaven face. He was dressed in a dark suit and his gray hair was slicked back. He looked like any other senior executive of a large corporation.

As we approached, Jimmy tried to introduce me but was waved off.

"Introductions are not necessary." Mr. Sullivan studied me for a few beats, rubbed his chin, then said, "William, please sit. Have some tea."

I sat down across from him and waited quietly. He

brought a cup to his lips and sipped slowly. The air was filled with the pleasant aroma of tea and honey.

"I've heard some impressive stories about you, William." He placed the teacup down slowly and brought his hands together on the table in front of him. "It has been brought to my attention that you handle yourself well."

A waiter brought a new pot of tea plus honey, milk, and biscuits to the table. Sullivan poured the hot tea into my cup; I added honey and milk and sipped carefully.

He examined me as I drank. "I have a problem and need your assistance. One of my associates has been relieved of his responsibilities. I would appreciate you filling his role."

I started to open my mouth, but he put up his hand to stop me.

"Here is a down payment toward our arrangement."

Someone to my right placed an envelope and keys in front of me. He was wearing too much cologne and it was so overwhelming I could taste it.

"Please, don't be too hasty," he said. "Give this

opportunity some thought. Come back tomorrow at this time with your decision and we will proceed."

I took the envelope and keys and shoved them into my pocket. I took another sip of tea.

A tall thin man dressed in all black approached the table from the right. I was immediately smothered in cologne again. Trying to identify the scent, spiced, citrus, I recognized it as Polo.

"This is Morgan. He will bring you up to speed about our organization. Please go with him and we will speak tomorrow."

I stood. "Thank you, Mr. Sullivan."

He studied me for a few seconds, then said, "Don't thank me yet, William. I know you'll make the right choice."

I followed Morgan further back into the bar and down a flight of stairs into a large basement. It was dark, but had a clean dry smell. Morgan hit a switch on the wall and fluorescent lights came on.

I followed him through boxes and cases of alcohol piled neatly against the walls to a door on the far end of the room. He took out a set of keys and unlocked it. We walked down steep stairs to another level. It smelled of old damp stone and dirt; the mustiness made me cough. There were other odors but I couldn't place them yet.

What I could place was a low moan and an animal panting; it sounded like a big dog. It wasn't a dog, it was a man. He was strapped to a chair in the middle of a large plastic tarp. Blood was coming from his nose, mouth, and fingertips. A stench filled the room, excrement, urine, and the metallic smell of blood. My stomach tightened and teeth clenched as I realized what was going on here. I recognized this method of interrogation. It was a torture room.

A huge, intimidating man with a shaved head, bloody apron, and rolled-up sleeves stood over the bleeding man. Teeth and fingernails were scattered on the floor in front of the chair. Various tools, blades, and hypodermic syringes rested on a table to the right. I swallowed hard to keep the bile down. Squeezing my fists tight, pure rage welled up inside me. I couldn't form a single word or sentence.

I flashed back to a mission in Afghanistan a couple of years ago. We were too late for one of our brothers, who had been strapped to a chair and slowly tortured for information. Pieces of him were scattered on the floor around his feet. We were trained not to give anything away about our base. Rank, serial number, and name was all they were going to get out of him and nothing else. The anger that I had buried from finding him like that was bubbling up. I felt that same rage from not being sent sooner to save him. It still sat somewhere deep inside my gut. I took a step forward wanting to kill this tormentor and end this horror show.

Morgan put his hand on my shoulder to stop me and finally spoke. "This is Bran Whelan. He manages our information needs." Morgan's voice was thin with a nasally pitch. It wasn't at all how I'd expected him to speak and I almost laughed.

Then Whelan turned and pointed a bloodied glove at me. "So this is the new guy?"

"Yeah, this is Bill Conlin."

An evil grin moved across Whelan's face. "You'd better watch your ass or you'll be next," he said. He pointed a pair of pliers at me, dredged up some phlegm, and spat.

"The show's over, Morgan. Get the fuck outta

here now. Giving away family secrets is unhealthy. Ain't that right, Rudy?"

Morgan looked at me. "Congratulations," he said. "You're Rudy's replacement."

CHAPTER FOUR

Jimmy was waiting for me outside. Kenny was gone.

"Mr. Sullivan is great, right?" he said, all excited.

"You're a fucking idiot, Jimmy. These guys are murderers."

"Come on Bill, its just business stuff. I do collections."

"Did you know?"

"Know what?"

"About that fucker Bran Whelan!" I screamed in his face and shoved him back against a parked car.

"I've seen him around. What's the big deal?"

"I met Bran while he was dismantling my predecessor, Rudy." I said, aggravated.

"Bill, I swear. How could I know?" he said,

turning a shade of gray.

"His fucking teeth and nails were all over the floor."

"Maybe they wanted to set things straight, you know, 'cause you're Army tough."

"I wanted work not a death sentence. Now I'm dead."

"Just follow the rules like me. You can do this. It'll be great."

"You're a fool, Jimmy, you know that? One wrong step and we're dead."

I was disgusted. I needed to get away from this place, from Jimmy, and from what I had just witnessed. Why would they show me that? It had to be a message of what would happen to me if I screwed up. I waved down a taxi and jumped in slamming the door. The driver took off.

"Where to, mister?" he asked.

"Just drive uptown."

I lit up a cig, and the taxi driver got upset. "You can't smoke in this cab."

"Stop here!" I shouted. I handed him a five and got out.

We went only a few blocks, but it was enough to get away from McKenzie's. How could I be so dumb? I remembered the envelope and took it out of my pocket. It was filled with hundred dollar bills. I counted the money and my eyes almost popped out. Five thousand dollars. There was also a note in the envelope with an address scrawled on it: 747 Tenth Avenue, 18J.

What the fuck was this, a setup? I hailed another taxi and headed to West 51st. It felt like I was dreaming. What was I getting myself into?

The cab pulled up in front of an expensive high-rise apartment building. The doorman stood outside wearing an official red uniform jacket with shiny gold buttons and a hat with a nametag: "Tony." He was smiling and staring at me while I stood there like an idiot. I didn't know what to say.

"Are you alright, sir?"

"I don't know," I said, with a confused look on my face.

He looked at me for a few seconds. "Can I be of service, sir?"

I looked at the keys in my hand and then back to Tony.

"I'm going in..." I began, but he cut me off.

"Allow me get the door for you, sir. Welcome to Hudson View Terrace."

I stepped into the lobby and was blasted by the coldest air conditioning I've ever felt. The floors and walls were made of red marble with gold veins. I could see my reflection anywhere I looked.

A guard sat at a cherry wood desk, a sign-in book open before him. He looked up as I approached. "Good afternoon, Mr. Conlin," he said. "Go right up."

At the eighteenth floor I got out of the elevator and walked down the hallway to apartment 18J. Should I ring, knock, or use the key? My nerves were getting the best of me. I didn't want to walk into a murder or another torture scene.

I took a deep breath, then took the keys out of my pocket and unlocked the door. When I pushed it open, a brunette with startling ice blue eyes, pale skin, and short black hair startled me. "I'm sorry, is this your place?" I asked.

"Hi, I'm Jackie. You must be Bill," she said, with a slight Irish accent. "Come in."

Jackie looked to be in her early thirties. She wore a

white T-shirt and no bra--her nipples showed through the thin cotton of her shirt. She had on red shorts with no shoes, and toenails painted red. She was attractive, but not really my type. Scratching behind my ear, I squinted. I was feeling perplexed. I guessed this must be my first job, though she didn't seem to have any problems with me being there.

I followed her into a large living room with modern furniture, a large flat screen TV on the wall, and hard wood floors. There was a hallway to the left and a kitchen on the right. Tall windows spread across the front of the apartment and led to a balcony. I peered out at an incredible vista of the Hudson River and hills of New Jersey. It was a fantastic view; I could see for miles.

"So Jackie, what business do you need help with?" I asked.

She laughed. "No business. This is your apartment and I come with it."

"You live here?" I asked, somewhat shocked.

"Aye, this is where I work and live," she said, with a coy smile. "Come on. I'll show you around?"

We walked down the hallway. There were two

other rooms on the right, a bathroom to the left. In the first room was a desk with a laptop, a chair, and a couch. The next room was a large master bedroom, with another bathroom, which had the same incredible view as the living room. There was a king-size bed, an armoire, and another giant flat screen TV. I headed to the closet and opened the door. I was surprised to find a giant walk-in, the size of the office. It was organized with racks and a shelving system. Men's clothes and accessories covered every inch of space; suits, shirts, ties and casual outfits. The back wall was shelved with shoes, boots, and sneakers.

I sat on the bed. I rubbed my eyes and sighed. Jackie came over and sat next to me.

"Rough day, huh?" Jackie asked.

I started to say something, but stopped. She undid my belt and pulled down my pants. "You need to unwind," she said.

I couldn't hide my excitement. I hadn't been this close to a woman in a long time. Her perfume smelled of vanilla and Jasmine. She laid me down then took off her clothes and straddled me, rubbing her soft, powdery skin and small perky breasts across my chest.

Things progressed quickly. We soon finished together, panting, sweating, and giggling.

I fired up a cig and we shared it. "Do you know Rudy?" I asked her.

She gave it a thought, then replied with a sad expression, "He used to live here, but has been reassigned."

Seeing this upset her I changed the subject. "What do you know about Mr. Sullivan?" I asked her.

"Stay on his good side, or you'll get reassigned too."

About a half hour later, I headed over to my crappy building to get some of my things. The smell of garbage and cooking almost made me gag. Once inside, I decided to crash out for a while and reflect on the day's events. After a while the phone buzzed. Jimmy.

"Hey," I said casually.

He was agitated. "Dude, you gotta tell me what's going on?" he said.

Sleep in my voice, I said, "I'll meet you at the pub in an hour."

Three hours later I was still in bed. My buzzer startled me awake. Jumping up I pressed the intercom button.

"Who is it?"

"You're gonna make me fucking come get you? You are such a fucking asshole. Buzz me in." Jimmy said.

I pressed the buzzer and unlocked the apartment door. He came rushing in and slammed the steel door shut. He took a deep drag of his cig, cheeks sucking in outlining his cheek bones, the cherry red tip glowing as it burned brightly in the dark room. Seconds later the room was filled with smoke and he came closer. A combination of whiskey and cigarette breath assaulted my sense of smell.

"Gimme the fucking dirt. Where'd you go and what's your deal?" he said.

"You're not gonna believe this," I said, then I replayed the day's events. He was riveted. His eyes, red and glassy, were glued to me; a cigarette hung from his bottom lip, defying gravity.

"That's fucking unbelievable!" he shouted. "Rudy must've pissed them off real bad!"

"I gotta find out what happened."

"Money before you even started. An apartment

and a horny tart." He paused again, taking it all in, and then blurted, "You are the man!"

I looked straight in his red eyes. "Yeah, I might just be a dead man," I replied.

He lit another cig. "How did Mr. Sullivan leave it?"

I rubbed my face and sighed. "He wants to see me in the morning with my decision. So I guess I get Rudy's job or something worse."

CHAPTER FIVE

Rudy appeared and he was yelling, but I couldn't understand anything he said. It was all gibberish. He attacked me, his hands around my throat. As we struggled on the floor, I grabbed a knife and stabbed him half a dozen times. Blood spurted and gushed out of him. I looked down at my hands; they were soaked with blood. The knife dropped to the floor.

Jackie let out a frightened scream, and then I shoved her into a green plastic bag. I wrapped it tightly with duct tape, but she was alive, kicking and wiggling. I could see the shape of her mouth opening and closing through the plastic like a fish out of water. She was trying to get air. She was suffocating. Filled with anger, I started kicking Jackie's head as she struggled to breathe. "Stop moving!" I yelled. "Stop moving!"

I continued kicking her head until she went still. Horror, fear, and guilt racked me as I realized what I'd done. I had to hide the bodies, but how was I going to get them out of Sullivan's apartment?

I suddenly became focused on my shoes. They weren't mine, but were new from that big walk-in closet. There was shit all over the bottoms. I took a few steps and turned to see that I had left a trail of shit behind me, all over the expensive floors. Wiping each shoe on the floor only left more stains. I became so frustrated that I took off the shoes to clean them. When I flipped the shoes over they were already clean.

I woke up in darkness, sweating and gasping for air.

My mind was stuck cycling like a broken record, repeating, "How can this be? They can't be clean!"

My heart was pounding so hard with fear I thought it would jump out of my mouth. I could still picture the shapes and images from the nightmare in my mind. The guilt and embarrassment of kicking Jackie to death clung to me. The green plastic bag and her mouth struggling for air burned in my mind, every time I closed my eyes I could still see her. Chills shook my body. Cold sweat soaked the sheets and the T-shirt I had been sleeping in.

I got up, changed, and walked to the kitchen to get some water. Jimmy was out cold on the couch, snoring loudly. Cigarette ash was all over his chest, a black-tipped filter sticking out of his puckered lips like a baby's pacifier.

"You drunk fucking idiot, you could've burned us down," I said under my breath.

I went back to bed and stared at the ceiling until sleep took me again.

When I woke the next time it was morning. I took a quick shower, made coffee, and changed into jeans, a white button-down shirt, and black boots.

My nightmare was over, but the anxiety remained. Mr. Sullivan expected me to accept his generous offer. I had no doubt that any answer other than yes would lead to Bran Whelan's chair.

Now I was chain-smoking as I paced like a caged tiger. I went into the bathroom to splash cold water on my face. I brushed my teeth, gelled and combed my hair, and looked in the mirror. I looked like I was about to pass out.

I squinted at my reflection. "You can do this," I said to myself. "Just stay cool."

Jimmy was ecstatic, puffing away and drinking already from a flask that he kept in his jacket. He looked at his watch and offered me a swig. I shook my head and continued smoking and pacing. For Jimmy this was like a Hollywood movie premier on opening night. He felt like the producer or agent, discovering my raw talent. He expected to cash in on whatever Mr. Sullivan's plans were. I was getting the feeling that he knew more than he was letting on, but he never clued me in.

Jimmy put his cigarette out in one of my coffee mugs. Looking frantically at his watch again, he said, "Let's go brother. Our ride should be outside."

Kenny was waiting at the curb for us, engine revving. I climbed into the backseat, and Jimmy jumped into the front, slamming the passenger door. Kenny gunned the engine and bolted out into traffic. A taxi screeched its brakes and swerved out of Kenny's way. I was tossed from side to side, sliding around on the backseat. Jimmy hung out the window yelling at people at the curb. "Get out of the fucking way, you idiots!"

This time both Kenny and Jimmy escorted me into McKenzie's. Morgan sat at the table where I had met Mr. Sullivan. As we approached, Morgan's cologne greeted me first.

"Mr. Sullivan will be here shortly. Please sit down." I still couldn't get over how nasal his voice was.

Eventually Mr. Sullivan and Bran Whelan came out of the back room. Sullivan signaled the waiter and took a sip from an imaginary teacup. The waiter nodded, disappeared, and returned with tea and biscuits. Jimmy started to light up. Kenny intercepted the cigarette, leaned over, and whispered something into his ear.

Mr. Sullivan addressed me directly. "William, it is time for your decision."

"I've decided to accept your generous offer," I said.

He began swirling a spoon around in his tea.

"That is a wise decision, William. Sadly, our friend Rudy was unable to remain loyal while working with some of our contacts. I hope you won't make the same mistake." Looking at Jimmy for a few beats, he added,

"Unfortunately, there are those who fall victim to temptations of our rivals. Jimmy has performed well with collections."

I glanced over at Jimmy, his eyes locked on the boss, nodding and smiling, proud of the pat on the back.

Mr. Sullivan then caught my eye and placed his hand on my arm. "Listen to me, William," he said. He paused for a few seconds, then began again. "We must maintain dominance over the West Side. We are constantly being tested. The Russians, Mexicans, and others probe us for weaknesses. These people have no honor, no respect, and no fear. For that reason, an example must be made. A show of strength."

Pausing again for a few beats, he smiled and added, "I'm a generous benefactor when my needs are met. I've demonstrated how good and bad behavior is rewarded. Our partners in Little Italy want this problem handled quickly. Things will settle down for a while after some trouble makers are dealt with."

He paused again and looked directly at me. "William, I expect absolutely no witnesses."

Then he finished his tea, stood, and patted my

back.

"Morgan is your contact," he continued. "He will supply information and all the resources you need. Don't come back here until this assignment is complete."

Sullivan left. Whelan gave me an evil grin, then followed Mr. Sullivan out, along with a couple of other men in suits. When my assignment is complete? What was my assignment? Morgan studied me, then looked from Kenny to Jimmy. "I hope you will excuse us gentleman. We have some things to discuss privately. Please follow me, Bill."

I followed Morgan upstairs and down a long hallway. He unlocked a door. Once we were inside, he closed and locked the door behind us.

In the room, a large map of the tri-state area hung on one wall. Different color pins dotted the West Side of Manhattan. Morgan unlocked a filing cabinet and pulled out a manila folder.

"There is a new leader of the Mexican gangs," he said, looking at the contents of the folder. "In the past they mostly fought among themselves. Recently, an Armando Sanchez has been organizing other Mexican gangs." Morgan then fanned out several black and white pictures of a man wearing a white sleeveless T-shirt with tattoos all over his neck and shoulders. He had a thick goatee and shiny black hair with bangs at an angle almost covering his eyes.

"Sanchez has been harassing our prostitution customers, and killed some of our employees. He stormed into one of our locations and shot the bouncer and two of our girls. Sanchez operates out of a Mexican Bar near 116th and Broadway. He manages a brothel around the corner. It's always busy and they service all types of clients. Your job is to keep an eye on him, and not get noticed. Learn his patterns and find a weak spot in his routine."

I looked at the pictures carefully. This was going to be difficult but not impossible. I wondered to myself how a white guy wasn't going to look out of place in Harlem, but I kept that to myself.

Morgan walked over to a closet and pulled out a briefcase, which he handed to me. "Your tools," he said. The briefcase seemed extremely light. What could be in this case that weighed nothing and would help me deal with such a dangerous man?

I didn't ask. I waited until I got back to my apartment to find out. Once inside, I set the case down on the kitchen table, lit a cigarette, and opened it. Fear and self-doubt clawed at me as I saw what I had been given: A steak knife, a large plastic bag, and a roll of duct tape were my only resources. I guessed this was another test to see if I had the guts and smarts to pull this off.

CHAPTER SIX

Later that evening I took the 1 train up to 125th Street to do some recon. I spotted the Tequila Lounge and Restaurant up a ways from the subway exit, and I headed up the street to a building opposite the bar. I starting pressing apartment buzzers and waited for someone to answer and buzz me in, but no one did.

Four men stood in front of the restaurant, watching the block, scanning in each direction. I guessed this wasn't a group of friends out enjoying a smoke, but guards. I realized I couldn't stay where I was standing anymore without looking odd, so I walked back up the block and found a pizza place. I sat in the widow and ate a slice while I watched the bar.

When I finished, I decided it was time to get a closer look. I managed to walk right by the men without attracting attention. The guards looked tough, tattooed with shaved heads, and they spoke Spanish. I headed into the Super Mini Mart next door to the bar and bought a pack of Marlboro Reds.

When I came out, I headed in the other direction and walked around the block. That's when I noticed an alley behind the restaurant. The entrance was blocked by a wrought-iron gate, complete with padlock. As I examined the gate, the sound of shoes on the pavement started getting closer. Panicked, I climbed over the fence and squatted behind some garbage pails that were standing against the wall. I heard voices getting louder as they came closer, and men laughing loudly. Night patrols. Looking around the alley I spotted a fire escape. I thought if I had to make a break for it, I could always go up.

I realized, hiding behind the trash that I needed a better way to find out about Armando Sanchez's businesses and activities. Watching from a distance wasn't going to cut it. I had to get closer to see what made this operation so successful and find a weak spot. The only way was to become a customer.

When I returned the next day, in the afternoon,

the atmosphere was much less threatening. The guards, gangs, and street patrols were all gone. I stepped inside the Tequila Lounge and was immediately overwhelmed by the aroma of beans, chips, and chilies. It made my stomach growl. A family-style lunch crowd happily enjoyed Mexican food. A couple of folks were at the bar having cocktails. I sat next to an old man munching on chips with salsa and sipping amber liquid in a short glass.

In a discreet way, I tried to make small talk. "Hi," I said.

"Hello, young man. My name is Hector."

"I'm Bill," I said.

He turned out to be an incredibly pleasant guy, friendly and talkative, and he offered to buy me a drink. Hector told me that he worked locally in construction and stopped here for lunch. I made up a story that I once dated a Spanish girl from Mexico, that she had left me for a Mexican guy once things started getting difficult.

"I loved her so much," I lied. "She was beautiful. Silky black hair, dark brown eyes, and a great body. She made me tortillas and chicken all the time. I fell head over heels in love with her," I said.

"Our women love to take care of their men. Cooking, cleaning, and loving with passion." He took a sip of his drink. "You need a new girl, my friend."

I sighed. "I lost my job, then we started fighting over money and she found someone else," I said.

"Yes, yes. I understand," Hector said, nodding with a sad expression.

"This is my girlfriend now." I said, showing him my right hand.

He let out a big hearty laugh, and then went into a coughing fit. When he stopped coughing, he spoke again. "There are ways to meet girls, my friend. So when you meet a nice girl you don't ruin it by being too eager," Hector said.

I wanted to appear lonely and pathetic. Looking into my glass, I placed a palm on my cheek.

"I have money since I started working again," I said. "But where can I find some girls?"

Hector got up to leave. "Speak to Luis, the bartender. He knows of these things."

I handed him a ten-dollar bill.

"Thanks, Hector," I said. "Please take this."

He stared at the money, then looked up at me. "No thank you, my friend. Give it to the girls."

On his way out Hector whistled loudly and pointed at me. The bartender stopped washing glasses and looked my way, but then continued his cleaning.

Luis stayed at the far end of the bar and didn't seem concerned about me once Hector left. Luis was in his early forties, balding with a comb over, and a belly that stuck out of his vest. I signaled him for another drink and he meandered over.

"Excuse me, but could you possibly help me out? Hector said you know where to find girls?"

"I don't know you," he replied gruffly, and gave me the once-over. "First you drink more, and then we talk about mamacitas."

"Beer and a tequila please," I said with a smile.

He gave me a look, then walked into a back room. After a while two guys with shaved heads and tattooed arms came over. One was short and thin, the other big and fat. The fat guy had to weigh close to three hundred pounds. They stood on either side of me.

"Is there a problem?" I asked.

The fat guy took my drink and drank it. "Yeah,

you got a problem now, *ese*," he said.

The guy on the left bumped me.

"Yeah, Holmes. You a cop? We don't like cops here."

"No, I'm just looking for a date," I said, my palms up and shrugging, trying to come off as nonthreatening.

"You wearing a wire?" the fat one asked and he started to pat me down.

"No wire here, Paco. But I don't trust this cop."

"Come on guys. I told you. I'm not a cop. I just heard you guys know where the pretty girls are."

"Oh, we've got hot mamacitas bro," said Paco. "But you gotta pay an initiation fee. White boy price is two knots to get in the club." He held out his hand.

"What's two knots?" I asked.

"Two hundred dollars, motherfucker!" he barked, agitated.

I reached into my back pocket and the fat guy immediately grabbed my hand.

"Whoa bro! Not now. Give it to Luis when he brings your drinks."

The two guys disappeared into the back room.

Luis came back with beer, a shot of tequila, a saltshaker, and a lemon wedge.

"That'll be two hundred thirty dollars, my friend," he said, smiling.

"How do I know you're not going to rip me off?" I asked.

"Maybe you should talk to the boys again," he said, the smile leaving his face.

"No problem. Let me settle things now," I said, giving him the money.

He counted it, put it into the register, and pushed a napkin across the bar. I flipped it over. There was an address on the other side, 660 West 129th Street. Written below were the words "Ask for Angel Eyes. Say Luis sent you."

CHAPTER SEVEN

I returned to the neighborhood several hours later. The address Luis gave me was a few blocks north of the Lounge, just past Broadway. As I approached, one of the guys hanging out in front of the building stood up and flicked his cigarette at my feet. "You're in the wrong part of town, *pendejo*!"

"Luis sent me. I'm here to see Angel Eyes."

He stepped close, got in my face, and stared into my eyes for a few seconds. Then he turned and pointed to a camera by a green metal door. "Tell it to the cam," he said.

I took a couple of steps toward the green metal door.

"I'm here to speak to Angel Eyes," I said, looking up at the camera.

After a while, the door buzzed. I pushed it open and entered. Loud thumping techno music filled the building. I was greeted by a large bouncer, a thick biker type with tattoos around his neck and arms. He had a headset on with a microphone, and stood in front of a chain-link gate that blocked the upstairs. On his left was a hallway with stairs going down.

I tried to peek around him but he moved in front of me and started to stare me down. I smiled and stepped back.

Looking down at a clipboard, he asked, "Name?"

"Alex. It's my first time at the club."

"No Alex on the list," he said, not looking up.

"Luis sent me. Told me to ask for Angel Eyes."

He pressed a button on his ear and started speaking. "There's a new guy here asking for Angel," he said. He paused to listen then opened the gate.

"Fourth floor office," he said and let me pass.

I headed up the narrow stairs and came around to a landing, where a guy sat at a desk with a small grey metal box in front of him. He pointed and I turned to see another set of stairs going up.

The music grew louder, vibrating the floor. People

cheered with excitement as a woman's voice urged the crowd to move their bodies to the music.

Up two more flights of stairs and another landing, two guys sat on either side of a door, with a sign that read *Employees Only*. Their arms were folded and they talked and laughed. When I approached, they stopped talking abruptly and stared at me with stone faces. One guy stood up and took a toothpick out of his mouth. "That's far enough, Holmes," he said. "That door is for you." He pointed to a door I had just passed in the hallway.

He sat back down and said something under his breath. I couldn't hear him, but he and his goon friend both started laughing. I headed down to the door they told me to go to. Out of the corner of my eye I noticed the door at the far end of the hallway had opened. Armando Sanchez came out with two guards, following him. He looked very different from his picture. His head was shaved and a thick mustache replaced the goatee from the photo. I recognized Fat Paco with him.

I hit the buzzer and the door opened. I entered the room and was patted down again by a guy I hadn't noticed was behind me. The room had big windows looking down two stories onto the crowded dance floor. Colorful lights flashed giving the room a magical glow. A woman in a windowed booth shouted into a microphone. She was dancing, waving her arms, and gyrating to the beat. After a while she turned and came out of the booth.

Her beauty stunned me. She wore a long black slinky dress displaying fantastic cleavage; and her breasts were pushed up and plump. She strutted over confidently, her dress swooshing with each step. She had beautiful black hair, long and shiny. Her eyes were dark brown and her skin had a tropical tint.

She flipped her hair. "Welcome to the Club, *hombre*. I'm Angelica."

"Nice meeting you. I'm Alex. Would you have a drink with me?" I asked, smiling.

"No, I'm sorry stud. You'll have to pick up your own girl downstairs," she said, winking.

I headed down to the second floor. A guy at the desk held out his hand. "Thirty dollars cover charge."

I counted out the money and handed it to him. He slipped it into the metal box and opened the door.

Inside, it almost looked like a regular dance club, but with no dance floor. Instead there was a center stage with twenty girls of different shapes and sizes dancing on a platform. Most were in bathing suits, others in lingerie, and others were topless with G-strings. They all held onto a pipe that ran around the ceiling, air-humping and gyrating to the techno music. Around the stage, mostly guys and a few girls watched.

A bar circled the stage and bartenders were cranking out drinks as fast as they could make them. Leaning against the bar I watched as guys went to the stage and handpicked girls they wanted. Holding hands, the girls stepped off the stage and led their clients upstairs to private rooms.

"What you having?"

"Two fingers of Knob Creek," I replied, and put a twenty on the bar.

A guy next to me leaned over. "You're new."

I sipped my drink and nodded.

"This place is better than having a girlfriend," he said.

"Costs a whole lot more," I said.

"It's only more at the beginning, with the starting

fees and shit," he said. "Then it's not so bad. I got all my friends here. No old lady to bitch at me. I can come and go when I feel like it and have a different girl every time." He took a swig of his beer. "If I don't like who I get, no problem. I just pick another girl. Ain't that right Eugene?"

"Fuck yeah!" said a guy to his right.

"I'm Roberto and this sorry sack is Eugene." He stuck out his hand and we shook.

"I'm Alex," I said.

"We work in demolition, gutting the abandoned building up on 136th," Roberto said.

"I've had a lot of these girls," said Eugene, leaning in. "Most are pretty clean. I've been coming here for a year, ever since that other place had a shoot out. Sometimes, I forget where I am, until I have to pay." He shook his head and started laughing.

"Oh, before I forget, watch out for Angel," Roberto said. "She's gorgeous and lethal. Armando's the head guy and her brother. He'll rip off your balls and make you eat them if you touch her. His crew is always patrolling and reports in constantly." He looked around, now suddenly nervous.

"Thanks for the tip, man. See you around," I said. I finished my drink and took a cruise around the club. There were definitely patrols and bouncers all around the stage.

I looked up to the booth where Angel spun out tunes and danced. I thought about what Roberto said, that Armando was her brother. I decided I had to get close enough to Angel to enrage her brother. His anger could be the key to bringing him down if I could catch him off guard. It was a fucked up plan, but I had to give it a try.

"Please send a bottle of champagne to the DJ up in the booth," I said.

He gave me a distressed look. "Not a healthy idea, my friend. Angel is off limits to clients."

"Just send it. I'm not a client yet and these girls aren't my type," I said, trying to sound irritated.

"Okay, it's your funeral," he said. He placed a bottle of champagne and ice in a metal bucket and carried it out of the room.

After a while, he came back.

"It's been delivered," he said.

I looked up to see if Angel was in the sky booth,

but it was empty. On the other side of the club I noticed a reserved section of tables and chairs. Armando and his crew were drinking and smoking, their watchful eyes scanning the club. A man walked over, put a metal bucket on the table, whispered in Armando's ear. Pointing in my direction, he said something and they all laughed.

The guy with the bucket came over. "Manny Sanchez would like a word," he said. "What's your name?"

"I'm Alex," I said, and I followed him to the table.

"So Alex. I've never had a gift sent to my table," Armando said, sizing me up. "Are you a queer or maybe this is something else? I like the gesture very much, please sit and let's talk." I took a seat.

"You are new, and don't like our girls?" he asked, narrowing his eyes.

"I'm looking for something different," I replied.

"Ah, something different, I see. Well first I'll give you a gift, have a cigar, *vato*," he said.

Manny opened a box of Cubans and offered me one. I took one and bit off the end. A crewmember came over and put a flame to it. I puffed until the cigar was lit, the tip flaring brightly.

"Nice quality," I said and puffed again. I blew out the smoke, and started to panic. I'm way too close now and this is too dangerous, just stay calm. I never thought I'd be in this spot so fast. How long could I keep this up? I need to get out of here and regroup.

Angel walked over to the table and gave her brother a kiss on his cheek. She turned to me. "I see you met my new friend," she said to her brother, still looking at me. "We have to find someone very special for him."

"Yes, we are sharing gifts," he replied, a big grin spreading across his face.

She held out a glass. "I love Champagne," she said, and Fat Paco immediately rose and filled her glass. He then plopped back down into his chair and fired up his own cigar. Smoke hovered around his round face as he lit it.

I watched Angel pucker her lips and sip from the flute. I couldn't take my eyes off her. I felt my mouth hanging open. I turned to Manny, his watchful eyes on me, anger clearly welling up inside him.

"I have an idea," he said. "Let's take a walk, Alex."

He got up. "Follow me," he said.

The guys at the table stood as we left the room. I followed Armando up the stairs to the third floor. He opened the first door and we went in. Inside was a main area with two couches facing five doors. The doors led to small individual rooms. Each room had a number on the door, and was locked for private use. Manny unlocked and opened the second door.

"We tame and train our new girls here until they feel sociable. This one's for you, Alex," he said, coughing up phlegm and spitting it on the floor. "I've had this one a couple of times. Sweet as honey and still has a little fight in her."

Manny dug in his pocket and pulled out a condom.

"Gotta be safe, Holmes," he said with a smirk and handed it to me. "Fuck this *puta* and prove you're not a cop. We'll wait here while you get your thing on," he laughed.

I entered the room and found a bed with a small end table, and a girl crying at the foot of the bed. She had straight black hair and was curled into a ball. Cigarette burns marked her arms and legs. I immediately felt sick, as bile rose up from my stomach. Sadness came over me. I'd seen this before, war stricken children abused at the hands of their captors.

"I'm so sorry" I said, as I entered the small room. She didn't lift her head to see who was coming in. She clearly didn't want to be here. This was more than a whorehouse. This was a sex-trafficking ring. I stepped further in and locked the door behind me.

"I won't hurt you, but we need to hurry," I told her. "And we need to make this look good or they'll kill us both. You understand?" I asked.

She looked up at me, tears in her red, swollen eyes. I had to get her to trust me. "What's your name and where are you from?" I asked.

"I'm Emma, from Dublin, Ohio."

"I'm Alex, from Manhattan," I told her. "Tell me what happened? How did you end up here?"

"The Port Authority. I thought I got a gypsy cab, but they brought me here and won't let me go."

"Do you have any lotion?" I asked.

"Lotion?"

"I need to put something in this condom or they won't believe us."

"There's lotion and lube in the end table."

I unrolled the condom and squirted some lotion in it, then put lube on the outside.

"Can you start moaning like we're having sex?" I asked her.

She nodded and we both started bouncing on the bed and making noise. After ten minutes of that we sort of looked like we did have sex, all messy hair and dripping with sweat.

"Listen to me," I told her. "I'm going to come back and get you. Please try to hang in there. You need to join the other girls downstairs at the club."

There was a knock at the door. "Come on Alex, you done yet? We're gonna have to start charging you."

I came out with the filled, shiny condom in hand. I showed it to Armando, then threw it into a nearby garbage pail. He looked at his men then went in the room, where he saw sweaty Emma sitting on the bed. She backed up against the wall, putting her head down on her knees.

He turned grinning.

"Alright Holmes! I guess we don't have to shoot you. Full membership is granted. Now you can call me

Manny."

I pointed my thumb in the direction of her room. "Can she be my regular girl? I think I'm in love."

"Okay, Alex," he said, slapping my back hard.

We headed back to the second floor, where Armando and his goons left me at the bar then went back to their reserved tables.

Paco came close. I could smell his sour breath. "Stay out of trouble, Holmes. Manny gets pissed off real easy."

He waddled away to join his crew.

I turned to face the bartender. "One Mexican beer, *por favor?*"

"Five bucks," he grunted.

I drank the beer fast and left the club.

CHAPTER EIGHT

I couldn't get Emma out of my head. That poor girl. No one deserved that kind of treatment. There was nothing I could do for the children that haunted me. Images of their faces flickered behind my eyelids in a slide show of pain, sadness and horror. I was helpless to rescue them as they were raped and killed by their own people, during a senseless conflict, but I could do something now to save this young woman. I had to speed things up and get her out of there quickly.

Finally home, I stripped off my clothes and took a shower, letting the water hit my head for an hour. I got into bed and stared at the ceiling, my hands behind my head. After a while I fell asleep then awoke to darkness and silence. The clock read one thirty. I bolted out of bed, got dressed in five minutes, "packed" some needed tools, and took the train back uptown.

I watched the club from a distance. At three in the morning Angel and Manny came out and got into a black Range Rover parked up the block. Several minutes later they drove off.

I knew I needed to follow them to complete my assignment, but tonight Emma was my first priority.

I held up my membership card for the hoods at the door and after a few seconds got buzzed inside. The giant bouncer still blocked the entrance and stared hard until I showed him my new membership card. He moved to the side and unlocked the gate.

"Thanks man," I said.

I headed up to the bar and flagged down the bartender. He put his hands on the bar in front of me and nodded without speaking.

"Mexican Beer and a shot of Knob Creek, *por favor*," I said.

Manny's crew sat at the reserved tables, while a few other guys sat in the bar drinking and laughing. Paco noticed me and gave me a dirty look, his eyes narrowing as he whispered to one of the other men.

I shot back the bourbon, turned to the bartender,

and waved him over again. "I'll take a whole bottle of Knob Creek," I told him.

He looked puzzled.

"That's one fifty for a bottle. If you make a mess of yourself the office is gonna be real unhappy," he said.

"No worries. I'm going to share it with my friends," I said, smiling.

I paid the bartender, took a big swig, and let it burn my tongue before swallowing. It warmed my chest and stomach.

Taking the bottle off the bar I strolled across the club floor and over to the restrooms. I pushed open the men's room door and went into a stall. The sour smell of urine was overpowering and the floor was wet with the urine of sloppy club members. I winced as the odor made me gag. I waited until the last guy finished and left the bathroom.

Moving fast out of the stall I grabbed paper towels from the sink and the dispenser. I crumpled them up and pushed them into the waste bin. I poured the entire bottle of bourbon over the contents of the waste bin. Then dropped in around twenty bullets I had stuffed in my pocket. I had saved them as souvenirs from my tour and never thought I'd use them again.

I took out my green disposable lighter and lit the top of the paper towels. The fire started crackling and spread quickly, flames rising as the garbage caught. The fire flared up, catching the towel dispenser above and the heat burned my face.

I walked out fast. I crossed the main club floor and waited. No one noticed the smoke coming from under the men's room door. I stood on the other side and waited near the exit as the bullets started to cook off. Gunshots could be heard in the bathroom and it sparked a riot. People ran for the exits, screaming and panicking. Some got knocked down and crushed under the stampede.

"HE'S GOT A GUN!" I screamed.

The staff, clients, and girls ran for the exit while Manny's crew headed to the restroom, guns drawn. As the bullets cooked off, the crew started shooting back at the phantom shooter. A few poor guys who were closest to the bathrooms were shot dead by the jumpy crewmembers. I ran into the hall and raced up the stairs to the third floor. I tried the door, but it was locked. A crewmember came down the stairs from the office.

"You're on the wrong floor," he said.

"Oh sorry. I'm looking for the other girls," I said.

"No other girls here," he said, starting to get suspicious. As he approached he reached behind his back for a gun. I stepped forward, grabbing his arm as it came around. We struggled for control of the gun. He elbowed me in the chin, and I caught another in the face. I crouched and swept his feet out from under him. He fell and the gun bounced, firing off a round that echoed in the hallway. I hit him in the face with all my force; his nose broke and he passed out. Sticking my hand in his pockets I found a set of keys. I threw him over the railing headfirst and picked up the gun, a squatty looking Glock. I placed it in my waistband and tried the keys. Time was running out. After several tries I finally opened the door to Emma's room.

She was frozen, panic all over her face.

"Hurry, we have to go now," I shouted.

She blinked in shock, then realized what was happening.

"There are other girls. You have to help them," she pleaded.

I unlocked four other doors and discovered a horrible scene in one of the rooms. A girl lay lifeless on the bed, her eyes vacant, mouth open, and head hanging over the side. Blood had drained from her wrists and pooled on the floor.

A total of six girls were rescued that night. All were in the same condition as Emma: drugged, sexually abused, and beaten. They still managed to get on their feet and run to freedom.

"Get the fuck out! Hurry!" I yelled.

They fled into the hall and down the stairs. Pulling Emma by the hand we stepped over the body of the thug I fought in the hall. He lay unconscious with blood all over his face. We blended in with the stampeding crowd, pushing our way out and into the street. People scattered in every direction.

I dragged Emma along behind me and we ducked down the stairs of the subway station. Waiting for the train seemed to take an eternity. Then I heard shouting and footsteps approaching. Two guys from Manny's crew jumped onto the platform guns out. I wasn't sure if they were looking for the girls or us. I shot them both with four quick bursts to their chests, dropping each man. The sound echoed, frighteningly loud and ringing in my ears. They fell, blood spraying from their bodies, and crumbled to the ground.

The silence was deafening. I felt a ringing in my ears from the lack of sound. I thought of a time in another place, on another continent when an enemy grenade landed a few yards from me. My ears rang, the ground shook and a soul-searching heartbeat filled my head. It left me reeling, with a hollow feeling to check my body to make sure I wasn't bleeding or missing any body parts. I couldn't move or think until I heard Emma's quiet sobs and my own panting.

Distant police sirens grew ever closer as I shook myself back to clarity and finally the train pulled into the station. We got off at 34th and walked to my apartment. I'd never been happier to be in the safety of that rundown building.

Emma took a shower and I set up a bed for myself on the couch, letting her sleep in my bedroom. The next morning, we took a cab to LaGuardia Airport and I bought Emma a one-way ticket back to Columbus. I gave her three hundred dollars and wished her a safe return home.

She hugged me. "I don't know what to say, but thank you for saving my life."

Patting and rubbing her back, I said, "I'll wait and make sure you're in good hands before I leave."

I watched as Emma walked into security, and joined a long line of waiting passengers. She had no identification, but I knew airport security would help her get back home. I walked out of the airport, grabbed a taxi back to Manhattan and fell asleep on the way back.

The club would be too hot for me to ever go back. I was sure Manny's crew would be looking for me all over the city, and I had to be careful.

CHAPTER NINE

I woke up in the taxi just as we shot out of the Midtown Tunnel. The driver was speaking low. All of a sudden I got an urge to see Dana. I leaned forward. "Excuse me. Can you drop me off at Bryant Park?"

The driver continued to speak into his phone.

"Bryant Park Grill?" I said louder.

"Hey pal! The least you could do is put your fucking phone down and let me know whether you heard me."

He barked something incoherent at me and went back to his conversation.

I couldn't believe this guy. He lives in our country, enjoys our freedom, and can't even understand how to treat people and be a decent person. His rudeness was starting to get to me. I took a deep breath, blew it out and looked out the window trying not to let him get the best of me.

Ten minutes later we pulled up at the grill and the

rude taxi driver told me how much I owed without putting his phone down. I paid him with a tip, but he still didn't take the phone from his ear or say thank you. I left his cab pissed.

I walked through the outside café and into the restaurant where the host, a thin, dark-haired man in his late twenties, greeted me with a smile. "Can I help you, sir?"

"One for lunch, please. Can I be seated in Dana's station?"

He looked down at a book with reservations and table arrangements. "One moment, please." He checked the outside area and came back after a couple of minutes.

"This way, sir."

I followed him to the outside tables that faced the park. He seated me at a small table and handed me a menu. "Enjoy your lunch."

I took a sip of ice water and studied the menu. I heard a woman's voice from behind me. "Will anyone be joining you, sir?"

I didn't look up from the menu. "No just me."

"Hey, I know you," she said. "You're that unlucky

stud from the park." She cleared the other place settings then asked, "What are you fixing to drink stud?"

"I really like your accent, it's kind of sexy." I said. "I'm fixing to have a Black and Tan, please."

"Okay, I'll be right back."

She came back minutes later and placed the beer on the table. "Things must be looking up for you."

"Well that depends. Will you have dinner with me tonight?"

It caught her off guard, and her expression changed as she considered the offer. A little embarrassed and confused, she studied my face. "You're name is… Bob? No Will. Sorry, I'm bad with names."

"Close. It's Bill. But I didn't forget your name, Dana."

"You got me there."

"Will you meet me tonight, so we can get to know each other?"

"Order and I'll think it over."

"Okay, I'll have the gazpacho and the fish and chips."

"Good choice. I'll be back in a sec."

After a while, she returned with the soup. Each spoonful tasted better than the previous. I wanted to lick the bowl.

"Wow. You did an excellent job," she said when she returned with the next course. She came by a couple of times to check in on me and then once again just as I was finishing my food. "So, how was everything?"

"The fish was awesome but the chips were soggy. Any chance I could get a refund?"

"Not a chance," she smiled.

I figured that was a good sign. "What time do you get off?" I asked.

"Tonight's not good for me. Call me tomorrow." She handed me a Bryant Park Grill card. I flipped it over, and already written in blue ink, in rounded, feminine handwriting was her name, number, and a smiley face.

She took my plate. "Call me at eight thirty tomorrow night."

I walked home, trying to clear my head. Dana's beautiful face, bright green eyes and vivacious personality had hooked me. I had to spend more time with her.

I called her the next night at eight thirty, just as she asked. We made arrangements to meet up at Mustang Sally's at nine for a drink. I got there early and stood outside, pacing and smoking. Finally she arrived, smiling that pretty smile as she approached.

We had a couple of beers at the bar. I couldn't take my eyes off her as I listened to her talk about her family in Texas and how she wanted to go back after she'd tired of the New York pace. I told her a little about my crazy cousin Jimmy chasing me to work with him, but I didn't say too much about the actual work we would be doing. Finally I asked, "Do you want to go someplace else? Get a bite?"

"What do you have in mind?" she asked.

I took her for a late dinner at Virgil's BBQ. We lucked out when we got there, as the kitchen wasn't closed yet. We sat on the second floor overlooking the bar.

Virgil's was a fun messy place to eat. The table had four squirt bottles of BBQ sauce in a carousel and brown terrycloth towels instead of napkins. Classic rock and blues music blasted as we stuffed ourselves on sloppy wings, dry-seasoned ribs, and kick ass margaritas. She liked reading, too, and we talked about books and our favorite authors. I told her some about my five-year tour in the army, but kept it light. She talked about her brother and how he was tragically killed while on tour. I thought about some of my brothers in arms that hadn't made it home, although coming home and being ignored and forgotten after laying down your life was no treat.

We left the restaurant and stood outside for a moment.

"You wanna come to my place?" she asked. "We can hang out, maybe see what's on TV?"

I gave her a sly smile. "Sure, but don't try to seduce me," I joked. "I'm not that kind of guy."

"Oh, I'm sure," she joked back, rolling her eyes. "Take a wild guess what I want to show you at my place."

"Is it your pussy... cat?"

She gave me a look, giggled. "Oh, you're a real keeper. No, that's not it."

We took the 1 train up to her apartment on West

72nd. She lived on the second floor of a walk-up, a clean one-bedroom apartment in an old building. It wasn't much, but still larger and nicer than my place. In the living room were a small couch and an old TV. Her bedroom had a floral comforter and sheets. Hung on the walls were framed pictures of flowers, and she had a couple of bookcases filled with fantasy novels.

"Over here is what I wanted to show you," she said, as she pointed to a collection of family photos. One picture stood out--a guy in a Marine uniform with a serious expression on his face. Next to that, a framed collection of medals.

"These are my brother's," she said, her eyes welling with tears.

A Bronze Star and an Army Commendation Medal for valor were part of the collection. These were the medals I had hoped for, but didn't get. I wanted to tell her more about what I had done and seen on tour, but didn't. Instead I put my arms around her.

"I'm sorry. You must be so proud of him. He was a brave man." I said.

She squeezed me back.

"He believed all people had the right to be free."

She said.

We sat on the couch and watched TV for a bit. I leaned over and breathed her in. She smelled nice. The scent of her perfume, light powdery and citrus. I softly kissed her neck. Taking in more of her scent drove me crazy. She turned and kissed me hard on the mouth. We moved to her bedroom and made love tenderly, with a slow rhythm that left me wanting more.

In the morning, Dana brought me breakfast. Eggs, bacon, toast and coffee. We hung out most of the day, watching daytime crap on the television, talking and laughing when I made fun of the soap operas. As it became late afternoon I started to get itchy. "I'd better get going," I said.

"When will I see you again?" she asked.

I gave her a kiss and walked out the door.

"I'll give you a call later," I told her. "I have some things to take care of. Thanks I'm really glad I had the nerve to ask you out and I want to see you again."

I started down the stairs, then stopped, and turned to see her closing the door. A sad expression crossed her face, as if she didn't believe me.

CHAPTER TEN

After leaving Dana's place, I stopped into Healy's for a drink. Glancing around, I noticed the same old faces.

"Hey Bill, where ya been?" Donnie asked.

"Working nights," I said. "Can I get a Guinness and a shot of Knob Creek?"

He turned to get my drinks. "Yeah, Jimmy told me you were working on something big," he said as he poured. He put the beer and shot in front of me. "Good luck. I hope things work out well."

"Thanks Donnie. Jimmy in today?" I asked, reaching for my shot.

"Not yet."

Just then, my chair went out from under me and I hit the floor hard. Pissed off I got off the floor and came face to face with Kenny's sleepy eyes.

"You've got some fucking nerve showing your

face here," he said, grabbing my shirt. "First I find you goofing off at your girlfriend's work and now you're here having cocktails. Living the dream, aye? What are ya on fucking vacation?"

"Are you tailing me?" I said, speaking through gritted teeth.

"I'm gonna visit your new your girlfriend, if you don't wrap things up fast.

"Leave me the fuck alone, Kenny."

"You could've got a gold star if you took out Armando fast, but you didn't."

"Couldn't do it yet. Things got complicated."

"Your assignment is not saving whores."

"Did Mr. Sullivan send you? Or, are you busting my balls for your own amusement?" I asked.

"Your dumb ass cousin is supposed to monitor your progress. He can't even do that, drinking all night and passing out."

"You asked Jimmy to follow me?"

"Rescuing girls and shooting Mexicans was not part of your assignment. Did you at least get your dick wet?"

"Did Mr. Sullivan send you to help? I was told I

had to pull this off with limited resources."

"No, he didn't send me. But I think he'll thank me later."

"I like that. It's like we're a team. You wanna be my sidekick, boy?" I sneered.

"You motherfucker!" he growled, grabbing my shirt and trying to knee me in the balls. I blocked it by turning to the side, tripped his legs, and threw him down."

He held onto me and we both crashed to the floor. I heard two loud metal clicks and looked up to see Donnie holding a cocked shotgun, pointed at us.

"Both of you assholes take it outside."

Once out on the street, I reached into my pocket, took out a green plastic lighter and fired up a cig. "You're fucking unbelievable, Kenny," I said, and blew out the smoke. "I don't need any of your crazy shit."

"When I saw you busted out with that girl, I wanted to shoot you myself. This isn't the Army where you can track terrorists for months and drop a bomb on them. Speed this shit up."

I rubbed the back of my neck. "Stay out of my way," I told him. "I'll track Manny and take care of business on my own."

Kenny handed me a piece of paper. "Take this."

I unfolded it to find an address in Fort Lee. "What's this?"

"I followed the Range Rover while you had your fun. Then came back, and found the streets buzzing with cops, emergency medical teams, and news reporters. Get your shit together or I'll finish you and make it look like an accident."

"Fuck off, Kenny," I said and walked off.

When I arrived at my building I noticed a brown refrigerator box on its side with a dirty off white comforter sticking out from the bottom. A metal shopping cart sat to the left filled to the top with green plastic bags. I came closer to the box and a head poked out of the right side. All I saw was a mop of gray hair and beard. Ronnie.

That's a surprise, I thought. Maybe I can give him a hand and get him back on his feet.

"Be careful son, they're here and watching you. I'll stay here on guard and report," he said.

"Good job, Ronnie. I need all the help I can get. You want something to eat or a shower? I asked.

"No thanks, I'll stay here and make sure no one flanks us."

"Okay, thanks. Keep up the good work."

I entered the building and ran up the stairs, blood pounding at my temples. Kenny sticking his fucking nose in my business had me reeling with anger. He was a loose cannon and I didn't like not knowing when and where he'd interfere next.

When I opened my door, I immediately realized something was wrong. The whole place had been tossed. The couch was gutted, the cushions cut open. The TV was smashed and the coffee table was shattered. I found Fat Paco sitting at my kitchen table with a gun.

"You fucked up, Holmes," he said, waving the gun. "Manny's gonna cut your fucking nuts off."

"How did you find me?"

He gave me a hard look. "I was at the subway station when you created that whole scene and killed my boys. They were stupid and too eager." He stood. "Now sit your fucking ass down."

When I didn't, he moved closer, and put the gun to my head. "We're gonna have a nice talk. Don't get cute. He paused, and then said, "Things are not what they seem."

"Like what? Oh, you mean that gun isn't loaded. Or, something else?"

"There's something you should know," he said.

"How much more of this guessing game crap is there?"

"Manny is not the boss, asshole. Angel is. She hides it well and uses Manny as the front man."

I grabbed for an open pack of cigs on the table. I slipped one out. "Want a smoke?" I asked. Reaching for my lighter, I flipped the table over onto Paco. Then I swung a chair at him, and he went down, out cold. The gun skidded across the floor and I grabbed it.

I smacked his face a couple of times. "Wake the fuck up."

He blinked and shook his head. "Let me explain," he said. "I gotta tell you something."

"You came here to kill or deliver me. That isn't happening now, Holmes." I pointed the gun in his face.

He held up his hands. "Don't shoot! I'm an undercover FBI agent working to bust a Mexican sex-trafficking ring."

My mouth hung open. "Why should I care?"

He wiped blood from the side of his head. "I know you care. You risked your life to save those girls, and almost blew a three-year investigation to find Angel's partners."

I took out the clip and popped the bullet out of the chamber. "Get the fuck out. I've got shit to do."

"Don't you understand? We need your help," Paco pleaded.

"All I understand is that you're fucking me up. I've got people following me and they're gonna want answers."

He slowly struggled up off the floor. I shoved him out the door. "Don't forget your gun, Special Agent Paco." I tossed him the gun and slammed the door.

Warkowski had been right.

CHAPTER ELEVEN

I left the apartment; Warkowski had moved his things across the street and up the block, but he still had a good view. I looked around for Kenny. I wasn't sure if he was still following me, but I needed to get to New Jersey in a hurry and find out what was up with that address he'd given me. But first I needed a plan and had to get a car. I'd seen enough car parking lots to know how they operated. I felt bad about stealing someone's car, but I didn't have time to mess around. Motivated by the thought of ending up in Whelan's chair, I went over to a neighborhood parking lot I'd walked past dozens of times.

I waited at an outdoor parking lot on 38th and Eighth, watching as parking attendants brought out cars and left the doors open while customers paid. I noticed an overweight businessman with a suitcase and shopping bags as he struggled with his wallet to get out a tip. The attendant pulled up in his tan BMW and ran off to get the next car. His wallet finally free, the businessman chased after the attendant, giving me a nice long gap. I jumped in and took off.

I headed west, right through the Lincoln Tunnel, then headed north toward Fort Lee. I parked in front of the building that matched the address, a large brick house with a double garage. I watched and I waited. At three o'clock the garage door opened and a black Range Rover came out. The windows were tinted dark and I couldn't tell who was driving. It looked like the same SUV I'd seen Angel and Manny leave in from the club. I followed from a distance for ten minutes. The Range Rover stopped at a school, with little kids playing outside, laughing and running around.

I saw Angel get out of the Range Rover and go into the school. After a while, she came out holding hands with a little girl, about four. The girl wore a flowery print dress and carried a baby doll that had no clothes on. She chatted and looked up at Angel with bright happy eyes.

They got into the Range Rover and took off, I continued to follow them. Next, they stopped at a McDonald's that had a play area. You could see the tubes and slides of the playroom from the outside. I parked a few spots over from them near the back of the parking lot. I watched Angel and the girl get out of the car and go inside; the driver stayed in the SUV.

I quickly walked over to the Rover and opened the passenger door. Manny sat in the driver's seat, and I shoved the Glock into the side of his head. He made a move for his gun. "That's exactly what I want. I'll blow your brains all over the windshield. Bits of your fucking brains are what they'll see after playtime."

I reached under the seat, and took the gun he was reaching for.

"What the fuck do you want? Money?" he asked, sweat running down the side of his face.

"Get out now and leave the keys for the girls. One move and I'll shoot you here."

I walked him to my car, and opened the trunk. "Get in." I ordered.

He gritted his teeth. "I'm not going anywhere, motherfucker."

I took out the Glock, and whacked the side of his head. He collapsed into the trunk. Then I duct taped his hands and feet and slammed the trunk closed. I got back in the car and headed south to the wetlands.

Killing Manny wouldn't be easy, but I needed to wait for dusk. Could I actually kill him in cool blood? I didn't know. One thing I did know, if I were in the trunk, he would have no problem killing me. I pulled over by an abandoned building and into the parking lot. No cars or people around, I waited a while for the sun to go down. I heard a thumping from the back of the trunk and knew Manny was awake.

"Let me out, you fucking asshole!" Manny yelled, his voice muffled in the trunk.

I should have taped his mouth. I got out of the car and walked around the back. Trying to get hold of myself and gather my courage, I leaned on the trunk and looked at the sky. I was fucked.

After a while, Kenny pulled up in his blue Ford. He got out and joined me at the trunk. "Seems as good a place as any, right Bill?"

"What are you doing here?" I said, under my breath.

He spat on the ground. "I'm your coach, remember?"

"No one said anything about you and me," I sneered.

"You show me yours and I'll show you mine."

He gave me a grim smile, and wiggled his eyebrows, staring at me for a few seconds.

"What the fuck are you talking about?" I said.

He tapped on the trunk. "Open it. Open it now, and let's get this show started."

I opened the trunk. Manny was lying on his side, shaking with fear and dripping with sweat. "Don't kill me. Please. I have money. You can have it. Millions of dollars and I'll take you to it. Please don't, please."

"You fucking kidnapped and tortured all those defenseless girls. You're a fucking scumbag," I shouted.

My mind went to a cold dark place. My feelings disconnected like I pulled a plug inside my brain. Old reflexes came back that I hadn't felt since the war. It was after I'd seen the casualties of war. How many girls had Manny killed, raped and tortured? This fucker had to die. I had to act quickly before my humanity came back and I became the hunted one.

I pulled a plastic bag over his head. Wrapped duct tape around his neck and watched as he suffocated. Manny struggled, gasping for air. He tried to bite the bag, but it was no use. His body convulsed for the last few seconds of his life then finally sagged. I stared for a while, numb from what I had done. Then took out my phone, and started taking pictures. Manny was dead and I needed to prove it.

"You got what you fucking deserved," I said to him.

Kenny patted my back. "Well done. I didn't think you had it in you," he said. "I'm surprised." He walked over to his trunk and opened it. Paco was in the trunk, duct tape over his mouth, hands, and feet. His eyes were filled with terror; tears rolled down his face. I couldn't believe it.

Kenny took out a gun and put it up to Paco's head. Muffled screams came out from under the duct tape. His chest heaved as he struggled to get air through his nose. Soon his eyes rolled up and he passed out. Kenny stepped away and put the gun back in his waistband.

"Let's get out of here fast. He can tell his friends all

about who snuffed Manny," Kenny snickered.

I took the tape off Paco's mouth, hands, and feet. He was still out cold when I yanked his fat body out of the trunk. He hit the ground hard with a thud, opened his eyes in pain and glared at me as I walked away. I opened the passenger door and got into Kenny's car and we drove off. Paco could take care himself, and I wasn't interested in helping him with his investigation.

CHAPTER TWELVE

I didn't go back to my armpit of an apartment. If Paco and his agents were going to pick me up, it would surely be there. I had to lay low for a while, stay at the uptown apartment with Jackie.

Kenny dropped me off. "I'll give you a call in the morning and pick you up to meet with Sullivan. Have fun," he said, grinning.

Jackie greeted me at the door in a T-shirt and panties, a margarita in her hand. Her nipples were showing through the shirt, but I was too numb to care.

"You look like a ghost," Jackie said.

I walked down the hallway and looked in the mirror at my colorless face. I had just killed a man, a bad man that would've killed me. The last moments before I put the bag over his head flashed behind my eyelids. His face suffocating, his mouth opening and closing like a fish out of water, struggling for air. What have I done? Panic, self-loathing and doubt pounded my brain. I headed into the bathroom and turned on the shower. The scalding hot water felt good on my face. I used a washcloth to try to scrub the murder away. I felt sick, dirty and evil. I scrubbed my skin raw, but it didn't work. I slid down the shower wall to the floor and let the water wash over me.

Jackie came into the bathroom and opened the shower door. She handed me a glass of bourbon. "I'll get you some ice," she said, and she headed into the kitchen.

I took a big swig of bourbon, and it made me cough. It burned the whole way down, warming my chest and stomach.

Jackie returned with a bag of ice.

"Are you going to be okay?" she asked.

I didn't move, but put the bag on my face. "I'll be okay in a few days," I replied.

She pulled open the medicine cabinet and produced an orange prescription bottle with a white cap. She opened the top and handed me a few pills.

"This should help you feel a little better."

"Thanks."

I recounted the day's events as the pills started to take effect and the guilt started to fade and I wasn't so sure I would make it out of the shower as my eyes became heavy. I woke up on the shower floor with my head leaning on the tile wall, the water still hitting me. I got up and stepped out of the shower, finished the rest of the bourbon, and went to bed.

I slept like a rock. No dreams and I woke up still feeling the pills in my system. Jackie had made some coffee and the aroma filled the apartment. I drank the coffee and lit up a cig. After the second cup, I started to come out of my haze.

My phone started vibrating. It was Kenny. I answered. "What's up?"

"I'll be there in ten minutes. We have to meet with Morgan and Mr. Sullivan."

I finished my coffee and got dressed. Then I headed downstairs and went outside to wait. Kenny was already there. He opened the car door and I climbed in. He gunned the gas and nosed the car out into the street.

"I hope you brought your phone. Mr. Sullivan's gonna want to see those pictures."

There was something different about Kenny, something that just didn't feel right. I couldn't place it, but he was treating me like I was something special. I wasn't sure if it was a good thing, but I definitely liked Kenny better this way.

"You impressed me yesterday, kid. Your cousin would have pissed himself," Kenny said. "Those Feds will be busting our balls for a while. I guess they still have their own work to do."

"What was your deal last night?" I asked him. "You were gonna let that agent suffocate in the trunk?"

He jerked the car to the side and pulled over, brakes screeching. He didn't look angry, but his stone face and sleepy eyes locked on me. "That's my fucking business, not yours," he hissed. "Bring that up again and I'll stick you and leave your body in the swamp."

I held up my hands. "Sorry, I didn't know you were so sensitive."

"Keep your fucking hole closed. Are we clear?"

"Crystal," I said.

He pulled out into traffic again, no longer in a

great mood.

A few minutes later we arrived at McKenzie's and headed in. Mr. Sullivan and Morgan were seated at the back table, already having a meeting. Five other men were seated with them, and they appeared agitated, locked in a heated conversation. I couldn't hear what was being said, but the men were waving their hands with animated gestures. None looked familiar. They had tough-looking faces, and were dressed sharply in dark suits, with colorful ties and shiny shoes.

They got up, shook hands, and walked past us. One tall thin guy, with a scar running down his right cheek stopped in front of me. He got up close and said, "This is your fucking fault, rookie."

Morgan signaled Kenny to come closer. He glanced at me. "Have a seat, Bill."

Mr. Sullivan poured hot water into his teacup. He slowly added a tea bag, honey, and milk. He picked up a teaspoon and mixed the tea in a swirling motion. Tapping the spoon on the edge of the cup, he sipped the steaming tea carefully.

Then he spoke. "Some of our associates are upset. It is as I predicted, William, and there will be more fallout from your first assignment. The Feds will attempt to shut down sex club operations all over town."

He paused, looked at Morgan, then continued. "The loss of profit will hit many of our people hard. This will cause some bad blood, but it will pass. The Mexicans have already hired a hit team that is looking for you. My suggestion is to lay low for a while until things settle down a bit. We have tipped the balance of power. Armando dishonored our organization and has paid with his life."

He held out his hand. "You have something to show me?"

I handed Mr. Sullivan my phone. Tilting his head to the side he looked down at the pictures. "This is sad, but a necessary evil." He handed back the phone. "Congratulations, William. You've proved your value. Stay sharp until this blows over and we'll be in touch soon. Morgan will settle things with you."

Morgan stood. "Let's go talk," he said. "Please follow me."

I turned to Mr. Sullivan, shook his hand. "Thank you for the opportunity."

"William, please be careful," he said. "Angel won't rest until she's evened the score for her brother's murder. Let her have the next move."

I followed Morgan to the second floor office. He closed the door and handed me an envelope. "There's a parking garage under your apartment building. Give this to the attendant," he said, and handed me a ticket.

"When you get back home, ask Jackie about the armoire. Stay alive and we'll contact you shortly," Morgan said.

I walked down the stairs and out into the street. Kenny was waiting outside, leaning on his car. "I'll give you a lift back to your place," he said.

We drove uptown to the apartment, and before I got out of the car, Kenny said, "Listen Bill, if anything comes up, call me."

"Okay, thanks," I said, and got out of the car.

I decided I didn't want to head back to the apartment yet so instead I took a walk to the west end. After a few blocks I came to the piers. I walked across the street to the terminal for the big cruise liners and stood there for a while, watching the water currents as the ships went by. As I watched, I wondered if the girls

I'd freed made it home or to a safe place. I wondered how long I had before the Feds and Manny's people came after for me.

Back at my building, I entered the parking garage and found a booth with a parking attendant. He opened the booth door, and asked, "Can I have your ticket, sir?"

"Here you go," I said.

He walked off and a few minutes later he drove up in a Lincoln Town Car. He held the door for me. I handed him five dollars. "Thanks," I said.

I pulled out of the garage and took the car for a ride around the city. I turned on the radio and tuned to a rock station. I started singing along to a U2 song, "New Year's Day."

"I will be with you again; I will be with you again…"

I thought about Dana and wanted to be with her, but wasn't sure about the dangerous people that were after me. I drifted back to the car; the new car aroma was wonderful and wouldn't last long. The Town Car was big, powerful, and bouncy. It felt like I was sitting on leather couch with wheels. The ride was as smooth as the leather. I barely felt any potholes. This car was absolutely awesome and kicked the crap out of Kenny's Ford POS. I returned to the garage after an hour and headed back up to the apartment.

Jackie was seated on the couch watching a reality show about rich housewives in California. I sat down next to her.

"How can you watch this crap?"

"Wait a sec, they're all ganging up on Vicky," she replied.

I got up, went to the refrigerator, and got a Corona. I sat down next to her again and waited for a commercial so I could get Jackie's attention. But within five minutes of watching with her, I wanted to know why these women were all being so mean.

"They are jealous of her success," Jackie explained. "She has her own money making business, is sharp as a tack, and doesn't need a man to define her."

"Can you tell me about the armoire?"

"Sure, what do you want to know?"

"Fuck if I know. *You're* supposed to tell *me* something," I said, getting agitated.

"All I know is that this is the key, and I'm not

allowed to open it," she said, and handed me a key.

I headed into the bedroom and opened the armoire. I couldn't believe how many weapons and explosives were packed in there. Shotguns, rifles, scopes and silencers hung on racks. Inside I found three drawers, each holding another grouping of weapons. One had knives, another pistols and ammo. The last had grenades and plastic explosives.

I stepped away and sat on the bed, staring at the open armoire. My mouth was dry. This was here the whole time, and I could have used the help over the last few days.

I knew holding on to the Glock wasn't a good idea. I didn't want to get caught without being able to defend myself, but now that I had this armory, I needed to get rid of the weapon that tied me to the murders at the subway station in Harlem. The cops wouldn't care that it was self-defense; since there were no witnesses I'd be locked up.

I took out a folding knife and a Beretta from the drawer. I loaded a few clips, threw the envelope in the drawer, and locked everything up. I would wait for dark then go toss the Glock in the River.

I headed out around ten. The air smelled of low tide. I strolled to Twelfth Avenue and headed south along the River. After about twenty blocks I came to a skate park by the water. I walked up to the fence and tossed the Glock into the river, then headed back home.

When I got back, Jackie was still sitting on the couch watching TV. A drink in her hand, she didn't move as I walked in and went into the kitchen. Opening the cabinet over the sink, I grabbed the bourbon and took out a short glass. I poured two fingers of Knob Creek, had a big gulp, and lit a cig. After a few swigs, I headed back into the bedroom, opened the armoire, and pulled out the envelope. I looked inside to see how much Manny was worth to Mr. Sullivan. I counted ten thousand dollars and had to take a seat. I'd never seen that much money at once before.

Being on Mr. Sullivan's good side was gonna make me rich, if I could stay alive long enough to spend it. I had no way of knowing how difficult this was going to be.

CHAPTER THIRTEEN

After a few days I tried to call Jimmy to meet me at Healy's, but he didn't return my calls. I pulled out of the underground garage and took the Town Car over to Healy's, hoping to find Jimmy smoking and drinking. I wanted to empty some beer bottles and knock back some whiskey with him. I grabbed a spot at the end of the bar, and then signaled to Donnie. He came over, took out a wet towel, and wiped the bar.

"How you doin', Donnie?" I asked.

"Okay so far, but it's still early. What would you like?"

"A Guinness and a shot of Knob Creek," I said.

When Donnie came back with the drinks he said, "Jimmy hasn't been around. Word is he's got Diesel issues."

I knocked back the shot. "What's Diesel?"

Wiping the bar, he leaned in, and said, "You know, heroin. I guess coke wasn't enough."

"When's the last time you saw him?" I asked.

"He came in several days ago, but he can't drink when he's shooting his money."

I ordered another round, thanked Donnie, and left a twenty-dollar tip.

I called Jimmy and his phone went right to voice mail, so I drove over to his place on 42nd and Twelfth. I pressed Jimmy's buzzer a few times, but no response. I took a deep breath and got back in the car. If he were out, he'd have to show up eventually, and if he were home, he'd have to come out. So I sat, watched, and waited.

After a couple of hours the front door opened and Jimmy staggered out. He looked bad. Thin, pale, and sickly. I opened the car door, then called after him, "Hey Jimmy, hold up. Where you been?"

He turned like he didn't know me. He quickened his pace and walked off. I followed after him as he turned the corner and headed into a building. A while later he came out slowly. He could barely walk and was a wasted wreck.

I grabbed his arm, pushed up his sleeve, and saw scabby bruises with needle marks. "Jimmy, you got a problem."

"Fuck you Bill. Stop hounding me. I'm just having some fun."

"So now you're a fucking junkie?" I sneered at him in disgust.

"Bill, you don't know shit."

"How long before Mr. Sullivan finds out and comes knocking?" I asked.

"I don't care," he said.

"Yeah, let's take a ride and get something to eat," I offered.

"Okay," he said, and I helped him into the car.

I took Jimmy to a diner on 42nd and we got seated in a booth by a window. The waitress, a cute, large-breasted redhead, came to take our order.

"Do you want to hear our specials?" she asked.

"Sure, go ahead."

She read us the specials, and I stared at her the whole time.

"What, no lobster?" I joked. She didn't think I was

funny.

"What are your boys having?" she asked.

"Cheeseburger deluxe," I said.

"I'll take some chicken soup," Jimmy said.

Jimmy was all itchy. He got up and went to the restroom. By the time he came back the food was on the table. He sat and stared at the chicken soup.

I took two bites from my burger, then said, "Sullivan is gonna have a serious problem with your state."

"Fuck him."

I took another bite, and looked up to see him nodding off. The heroin was in full effect, from his trip to the bathroom. He started to say something then faded mid-sentence. He tried to speak but couldn't. His eyes wouldn't stay open. It was a pitiful site. The old Jimmy was bad enough, snorting, smoking, and drinking, but he seemed to function. This was worse, more like the walking dead. I stared at him and wondered how long before this dose wore off. "How's your soup?" I asked.

He lifted his head for a second, smiled, and dropped it down again.

"Jimmy? How's your soup?" I asked again.

"It's real good," he said, and nodded off.

The waitress came back and put the check on the table. "Your friend doesn't look so good," she said.

"Yeah, he's having a bad day."

We walked to the front of the diner. I paid the cashier and left a tip on the table. Jimmy had made his way outside and looked like he was trying to go somewhere, but it wasn't working. He took a few steps, and then he started to fade, sitting in an invisible chair. I helped him walk back to the car.

When we got to his building, I helped him into the elevator and we headed up to the third floor. The apartment was a wreck, nasty half eaten bits of food, pizza boxes and garbage littered the living room. Dirty dishes filled the sink, plates were caked with food. I put Jimmy in bed and went to the bathroom. Used syringes and needles were scattered on the sink, and small empty drug bags were scattered on the floor. The toilet and bathtub had brown stains. The place hadn't been cleaned in a long time. Ashtrays loaded full with cigarette butts littered every room.

I plopped myself down on the couch, disgusted. I

needed a plan to get Jimmy back on track. Rubbing my forehead, I tried to figure out what to do with him.

I turned the TV on and got comfortable. I decided to stay the night to keep an eye on Jimmy, and slept on the couch. When I woke up and went to the bathroom, I found Jimmy on the floor, a needle sticking out of his arm. Foam and drool dripped from his mouth, and his eyes rolled up as a seizure racked his body. "Fuck! Fuck! Jimmy hang on!" I shouted, panicking. I ran to the living room and called 911, the phone shaking in my hands. I unlocked the front door and ran back to the bathroom and held Jimmy until an ambulance arrived minutes later. The EMTs immediately rushed in, ordered me out of the room and went to work on Jimmy. They took him out on a stretcher.

"Where are you bringing him?" I asked.

"Saint Vincent's," one of the guys replied.

I followed them out of the apartment but lost them on the way to the hospital on Seventh Avenue. When I finally got there, I headed for the reception desk, where a heavyset black woman sat behind a window.

"Can I help you?" she asked.

"Yes, my cousin James Campbell just came into the emergency room."

"Please take a seat, sir. A doctor will speak to you shortly," she said.

The waiting room was packed with people with assorted injuries. I looked up at the TV and mindlessly stared at the news.

When I saw the cops arrive, I realized I couldn't stick around for an interview, so I left.

Jimmy was in the hospital for a few days. The doctors put him on Methadone and sent him to a rehab center in Harlem.

A week later my phone buzzed. It was Jimmy from a blocked number.

I answered the phone, and he said,

"Hey Bill, it's Jimmy."

"You okay?" I asked.

"Yeah, better now. I owe you big time for saving my life."

I heard him crying on the phone.

"I know it was a mistake. I know it's all fucked up now." He said.

"You gotta fix your life. Sullivan isn't gonna let

you back in until you do."

"I'll fix things, you'll see. I promise."

A few days later, I was at Healy's, passing time drinking and talking with Donnie. Kenny came in and took a seat next to me.

"I'll have a Bass Ale," he said to Donnie.

"Your cousin is out of the crew until he gets cleaned up," Kenny said to me. "Mr. Sullivan doesn't trust junkies."

I drank the rest of my beer, and gave Kenny a dead stare.

"I'm not sure he'll ever be completely reliable," he said. Kenny put down an empty glass, and leaned in. "They want you to stay out of trouble for a while longer. Morgan said he wants us to partner up on a job, but not just yet."

"Let me know when and I'll be ready," I said.

He put a twenty on the bar and left.

Something didn't seem right. I didn't trust Kenny, so I decided to follow him. I waited a minute or two and walked out after him. I drove around the block until I spotted Kenny, sitting in his Ford and talking on his cell phone. When he pulled out, I followed him to an Argentinean steak house on the Lower East Side. This wasn't our territory; it was where the Columbian gangs sold heroin to rich kids from the suburbs. It occurred to me that Kenny had probably gotten Jimmy started on heroin to get him out of the way. That motherfucker could've killed Jimmy and what the fuck was he doing here?

Kenny headed into the steak house. A few minutes later, Angel sauntered by, wearing dark sunglasses and carrying a briefcase. She opened the door and went into the restaurant.

Why would Kenny be meeting with Angel? Kenny had to be a rat, and if Sullivan found out, he would end up like Rudy. The Mexicans were being tipped off about Sullivan's brothels. They terrorized customers, killed some staff, and busted it up. Now they were the only game on the West Side. I might have slowed them down a little, but the club was probably cranking again.

Why didn't Kenny kill Paco? The whole thing with Paco taped up in Kenny's trunk. It just didn't make any sense. Was Kenny an agent, a rat, or just an informant? Was he playing every angle? I needed to find out what was going on without tipping them off.

I turned off the car and headed toward the steak house just as a siren went off and two cars pulled up. I felt cold metal against my neck

"Get on the floor now and don't you fucking move."

I didn't resist. An agent handcuffed my hands and loaded me into the back of a black sedan. I was taken to a precinct and locked in a cell.

After a few hours, I was moved to an interrogation room. The room was small, with a large two-way mirror, and a desk, with two chairs on either side.

Two suits came in. One guy was tall and thin with bad skin. His wrinkled suit was dark blue, and he sipped coffee from a paper cup. He eyeballed me for a few minutes before speaking.

"I'm Agent Clark and this is Agent Burns," he said. "Do you know anything about the subway station shootings in Harlem? Two people died and a building was set on fire."

"I don't know anything," I said.

Agent Burns stood behind me. He leaned over and whispered in my ear. "So you're some kind of vigilante? Shooting up Harlem, setting fires and saving kidnap victims."

"Oh yeah, we know all about you, William Conlin," said Clark. "Big war hero, back in the states. Bored out of your mind. You should have signed up for the Police Academy when you came back."

"I have no idea what you're talking about," I hedged. "Am I being charged with something?"

"We want you to help us nail Angel Sanchez," said Burns.

"Who's Angel Sanchez?" I said.

There was a knock at the door and both suits walked out of the room. A few minutes later another guy came in. Fat Paco.

CHAPTER FOURTEEN

Paco took a pack of cigarettes from his jacket and fired one up. "You fucked things up, Holmes," he said, blowing smoke in my face.

"Is Kenny on your payroll?"

"Good question, but I'm not gonna answer that," he said.

"He got my cousin hooked on heroin, and it almost killed him."

"Yeah, well, shit happens," Paco said.

"Shit happens? Is that the best you can say?" I asked, through gritted teeth.

"It's a risk we were willing to take."

"If you're not gonna charge me, then fuck off," I barked.

"We could charge you with the murder of

Armando Sanchez."

"Go ahead," I shouted.

"Take it easy, Holmes. We can't do that just yet. It would blow the whole operation."

"What about Angel? She's gonna go to war after losing her brother," I said.

"Who do you think she's going to war with?" he asked.

"Sullivan," I replied.

He took a deep drag of his cigarette, and blew out the smoke. "That's the wrong answer. Her brother was shot in Jersey and she'll be looking for answers there. Besides, her brother hit Sullivan's whorehouse and everyone knows that the Irish would never let them get away with that."

"So, where does that leave us?" I asked.

"Look, Bill, you saved my life. I mean I probably would've suffocated if you hadn't helped me and I'm thankful for that. These other agents want to send you back to Angel to stir things up. I'm not going to let that happen, she would just kill you," Paco said.

"Where does Kenny fit in?"

"Kenny made a deal with Angel to share information about Sullivan's brothels. She's wants control of all prostitution on the West Side. Her connection in Mexico is what I'm after. They send her fresh product every month. She also has men watching the airports, train and bus stations, looking for runaways," he explained.

"Yes, the girl from Manny's filled me in," I said.

"So, we have an understanding. For now. You're gonna keep quiet and we won't put you away for the rest of your life, but…"

"But what?" I asked.

"Let me point it out again. One leak and its life in prison for you. Don't be surprised when we call you to help. You are free to go."

I walked out of the precinct and into the night. I found myself on 20th and Eighth. The agents had confiscated my weapons, leaving me vulnerable. Police cruisers were parked at angles all over the block. Patrolmen were clustered out on the street, telling stories and laughing.

I strolled over to a Starbucks on 23rd. As I opened the door, the combination of freezing air-conditioning and coffee aroma was intoxicating. I ordered a latte with an extra shot and sat in a cushioned chair.

As I sat sipping the coffee and looked around. Small groups of people were chatting, eating desserts, and drinking coffee. A couple of loners worked on laptops. I was envious of these people having their normal lives, where they didn't have to look over their shoulder.

How could I continue to do assignments for Sullivan with the FBI up my ass? Kenny was going to be my new partner. He was unpredictable before, but now I had to worry about him ratting me out to the Mexicans, FBI, or Sullivan. He was always a crazy bastard, but this made it worse. Kenny was playing every side, and I needed to make sure I was far away when he went down.

I took a cab back to my car on the Lower East Side and noticed a parking ticket tucked into the wiper blade. As I grabbed the ticket, I noticed a shadow passing behind me. Then I saw a bat coming at my head in the window's reflection. I ducked out of the way as the bat shattered the window, shards of glass flying everywhere. I kicked my attacker's legs out from under him, and he spilled to the ground. We both scrambled to our feet, and moved onto the sidewalk. He came at me again, but this time I was ready for the swing. Jumping back, I moved in fast with a punch to his solar plexus. His breath came out in a big rush of air, the bat falling onto the pavement. While he was still gasping for air, I kicked him in the face. Blood sprayed out of his nose and mouth, and he collapsed to the ground.

A white van came to a screeching halt by the sidewalk and the side panel slid open. Machine pistols sprayed the street and cars. People screamed and sprinted for cover. I dove behind a parked car and crawled a few feet. The white van pulled up to follow me as the shooters reloaded.

I raced back to the Lincoln, started it up, and pulled out. Flooring the accelerator, I rammed straight into the back of the van, knocking one of the shooters out. I backed up and rammed it again. This time the van scraped against the parked cars. I stomped on the gas, the engine roaring to life, and I maneuvered out into traffic.

I just barely made it off the block when three

police cars came wailing onto the scene, their sirens screaming and lights pulsing. I watched the police cut off the van from my rearview mirror. The shooters opened fire on the police, then more police arrived. I raced to the West Side, weaving through traffic, and sailed uptown.

When I pulled into the garage, the attendant greeted me with his mouth hanging open. His face was frozen with shock as I handed him the keys to my car with its nose pushed in, windows shattered, and bullet holes sprinkled across the driver's side.

"Wow, what happened?" he asked.

"I had an accident and they were pissed. What can you do? I'll get it fixed," I said.

"This was a new car, man," he said, taking off his hat and scratching his head.

"Yeah, it's a shame. I'll call a tow truck in the morning. Let's keep it low," I said, and handed him a hundred dollar bill.

Up in the apartment, it was dark and quiet. Something didn't feel right. Kenny turned on a lamp by the couch.

"What took you so long?" he asked.

"Where is Jackie?" I asked, panic in my voice.

"I sent her out, so we could talk," he replied. "If you fuck with my game, I'll skin your little uptown girlfriend."

"You've got fucking balls coming here. You touch her and I'll fucking skin you. What the fuck did you do to Jimmy? You got him hooked on heroin," I said, and took a fast couple of steps towards him.

That's when I noticed he had a gun out on his lap. He began to tap it on his thigh. "Like I told you before, we're partners now. I wanted to make sure you understood the consequences of crossing me," he said.

"Listen Kenny, I'm in just as deep as you. I just fought off a fucking Mexican hit squad," I said.

"Yeah, I told Angel where your car was and she gave me this." He held out a briefcase.

"So now you're trying to get me killed?"

"I figured, if you're as good as everyone says, then you'll make it out and I'll share this with you," he replied with a smirk.

"You've lost your mind, Kenny. I didn't even have a weapon." He lifted the briefcase and put it on the table. "See? That completely proves my point. Now stop being mad, come over and check out this out."

He opened the case. There must've been fifty thousand dollars in it.

"Holy shit!" I said, and plopped down on the couch in shock.

"I know, isn't it awesome? That Mexican babe Angel has a real wet spot for you. Here, take your half."

He counted out a large pile of cash, put it on the table, and closed the case. This was more money than I ever made in a year.

Kenny got up. "We're just getting started, partner. I'll see ya tomorrow."

Kenny left and closed the door. The apartment became quiet, and a chill went down my spine. I put the money in the armoire and grabbed a different gun. I took another Glock, a couple of clips, and a knife. The gun felt good in my hand and was a smaller gun than I was used to.

Kenny's plans would either get me rich, killed or both.

I headed into the bathroom. Jackie came back while I was still in the shower.

"I hate that fucking asshole. What did he want?" she asked thorough the door.

"I don't have a choice. Mr. Sullivan paired me up with him and now we're best buds," I said.

"Yeah well don't trust him. He was Rudy's partner before he was reassigned," she said.

She left the room. After a while she came back with a drink in her hand. She took a sip and lit up a cigarette.

"Kenny had Rudy running all over town," she said. "He set him up with the Russian, then tried to get him killed, then collected money from both sides. When things got too hot, he turned him in to Sullivan and blamed him for the whole thing. They didn't believe Rudy and he was blamed for everything. Kenny made it seem like Rudy was ripping off Sullivan."

I opened the shower door. Jackie let her clothes fall to the floor, and got into the shower with me. We fucked hard and fast, grunting like animals until she climaxed, then I did too. Exhausted, I sat on the floor. Jackie joined me, and we let the hot water roll over us.

CHAPTER FIFTEEN

The next day I went to check on Jimmy. He was being treated at a rehab center on the Upper East Side. The facility was all locked down, with metal doors at the entrance. The waiting room reminded me of a doctor's office, without the alcohol smell. Wall-mounted TVs were at either end of the room, with magazines on small end tables.

While I waited, I watched the news. The TV was muted, but I read the closed captions. A story about a car bomb in the Middle East was followed by a local news story--police activity on the Lower East Side of Manhattan. Three men shot at police and were killed, all believed to be part of a Mexican cartel involved in recent sex trafficking. "That's fucking great." I said, then covered my mouth and scanned the waiting room to see if anyone noticed. No one glanced my way.

The receptionist called my name. I was buzzed through the metal door and headed up to the third floor. Two nurses sat at a desk, working on computers. One was a pretty, older Latino woman, the other a heavy black man with a round face. The Latino woman stopped her typing and looked up.

"Can I help you, sir?" she asked.

"I'm here to see James Campbell," I said.

"James is cleaning his room and making his bed. I'll show you to the visiting area, and send him over when he's done," she said, smiling.

Jimmy cleaning his room and making his bed? Now this was a change. He must be miserable.

I followed the nurse to a large room where visitors and patients sat at tables on chairs with bright-colored seats. It was easy to tell who the patients were, they wore blue pajamas. Most of the visitors were parents of young adults in the program.

I sat and waited for Jimmy. When he got there, I noticed he looked better than ever, with clear eyes and a healthy color to his face.

"Dude, you've never looked this good. How are

you doing brother?" I asked.

"I'm okay, but you gotta get me out of here," he pleaded.

"Are they giving you anything to help you feel better?"

"I get a few different drugs. They're giving me something to help me focus, a mood stabilizer and methadone." He paused for a few seconds. I thought I'd lost him, but he recovered. "They won't let me smoke or go outside and they're making me clean my room," he said.

A faraway look passed over Jimmy's face. "I met a girl," he said, a little embarrassed.

"A girl? In here? C'mon? That's fucking awesome!" I said, and squeezed the back of his neck.

"She's over there. Her name is Tracy. I really like her a lot," he said, pointing and waving as they locked eyes.

She looked a little too young for Jimmy. Tracy was in her late twenties, with shoulder length wavy reddish brown hair. She was thin, with a pleasant face and average features. I looked and waved. Her parents in their early fifties didn't seem amused. Her dad had a little gray in his sideburns and gave us a dirty look. Tracy's Mom grabbed her hand and stopped her from waving.

"She looks real nice. Don't screw it up. Hey, you want some books?" I asked.

"I haven't read a book since school. Comics were always my favorites," he said.

"I'll go down to Midtown Comics and pick some up," I said.

Nervous and fidgety, he twisted the bottom of his shirt. "How are things going with the new job for Mr. Sullivan?" he asked.

"It's the weirdest job I've ever had. More money than I know what to do with and people trying to kill me all the time. Other than that, it's awesome," I replied. "Be happy you're out of the game, Jimmy. Kenny is all over me, and he's completely lost his mind."

Jimmy scratched stubble on his chin. "You know something? Now that I think of it, he went all crazy when Rudy was his partner," he said.

We talked for a while about old times and how much he wanted to get out. Then it was time to leave. I gave him a hug. "I love you man, hang in there and this will be over before you know it," I said.

After I left the rehab, I hailed a taxi and went over to see Dana at the Bryant Park Grill. I asked to be seated in her station. The host sat me inside at a small table. Dana came over. She didn't look thrilled to see me.

"What are you doing here? I gave up on you ever coming back," she said.

"I'm so sorry, Dana. I feel like that's all I ever say, but I've had some serious work issues. I can't wait to go out and spend some time together," I said.

"Is this some kind of weird head game? I thought you didn't want to see me anymore," she said, pouting.

"I can't get you off of my mind. Are you busy later?" I asked.

"Come by my place at eleven tonight, but if you ditch me again I'll find someone else to go out with," she said, narrowing her eyes, a scowl on her face.

I ordered some pasta and a beer, and I watched as she worked her tables. I wished things could be normal, but I had to see her even though it wasn't safe. I had no way of knowing if someone was following me and I couldn't tell her why I had disappeared.

She brought me the bill. I paid and gave her a big kiss. "See you later," I said.

She turned her face to the side and gave me her cheek. "We'll see stud, you're still in the dog house."

I walked out into the street. Waiting for me at the curb was Kenny in his blue Ford. He rolled down the window. "Wow, she's a real looker Bill. You'd better treat her right or she'll find someone else. Now, get in, I need your help."

I was barely in the car when Kenny gunned the engine and pulled out into traffic.

"Where are we going?" I asked.

"We're going to pay a visit to some people that owe me money," he replied.

He drove until we arrived at the same street as the drug house where Jimmy bought his dope. We sat in the car, waited and watched as clients came in and out.

"Why are we here?" I asked.

"We have to get Mr. Sullivan some money. I thought this would be a good place to start," he said.

This felt all wrong. "We're gonna rip off these dealers? Are they Mexican or Colombians?"

"They're fucking scum and we're taking them down. Now go over there and buy some junk," he said.

"Are you trying to get me killed again?"

"No, just get going and I'll back you up."

I got out and crossed the street. Kenny followed me a few feet behind. As I walked over to the guys at the door, they seemed to recognize me. One guy said something in Spanish and I heard Angel's name at the end. They started to reach for their guns when I heard two fast, muffled popping sounds. Kenny shot both of them in the head, a silencer at the tip of his gun. I pulled the Glock from my waistband and held it in front of me. These guys had to be Mexicans, the connection to Angel was clear.

Kenny took the lead and went right into the building. Inside, it was dirty and dark. We went up the stairs, to the second floor. Kenny knocked on a door. "Hey man, I was here last week and I wanna score some more. You got anything, bro?" he asked.

A guy cracked the metal door open, keeping the chain lock on. "Yo dawg, where you been? You want another eight ball?" he asked.

"Yeah," Kenny said.

The guy stuck his finger through the crack. "Hand over the money first."

Kenny moved so fast, I had no time to help. He kicked the door breaking the sliding chain lock and sent the guy flying into the room. Inside Kenny quickly shot everyone in the apartment. No one had a chance to even get off a shot.

"Come on, Bill!" he shouted.

There was blood all over the floor. The guy by the door was shot against the wall and two more people were dead in the kitchen. One guy on the floor was shot in the throat. Blood poured over the front of his shirt. A girl was dead in a chair, head back with a bullet wound under her eye.

"Look around, there has to be money and dope somewhere," Kenny said.

Kenny went into another room off the kitchen and started throwing stuff around. I pulled out the drawers in the kitchen, but didn't find anything. In the pantry, I noticed large cereal boxes and dumped them out on the kitchen table. The only thing that came out of the boxes was cereal. Under the sink were cleaning products and bottles of alcohol, mostly tequila and rum. I heard Kenny yelling something from the other room, but couldn't make it out. I looked in the freezer and found two large freezer bags of dope. One was filled with black tar heroin, the other was coke.

"I found it," I yelled.

Kenny came rushing in with a gym bag, packed with something heavy. "Come on we gotta go," he said.

As we came out, guys were waiting for us in the hall and on the stairs. Bullets started flying off the door and walls. We ducked back into the apartment.

I hope you're ready. This is gonna be good," Kenny said.

"Hold up," I said, and started looking out the windows until I found a fire escape. "Tell them we give up and we're coming out with no guns," I said.

He gave me an incredulous look. "You've got to be joking," Kenny said.

"Listen to me. There's a fire escape off the bedroom. Let's make a run for it. No one's out there. Going out the front is suicide," I said.

I went to the window, opened it and stepped out onto the fire escape. Kenny shouted something in Spanish and then came running to the window. We climbed down, our feet echoing off the metal of the fire escape. When we almost reached the street, they started shooting from the window. I laid down suppressive fire, shooting in short bursts, as Kenny made a run for the car. He pulled the car up, tires smoking, then jumped out and fired at the window until I got in. Kenny peeled out as bullets shattered the back and side windows.

He looked at me with a big grin. "Those Mexicans are tough on cars," he said.

"I thought they were Colombians."

"Nah, they just buy dope from the Colombians and then sell it here," Kenny said.

We drove across town with four motorcycles roaring behind us. As soon as they caught up to us, they started shooting. Bullets ricocheted off the car and I ducked my head down. I pulled my Glock out and returned fire out of the back window. One of the motorcycle assassins went down, his bike flipping over parked cars and into a flower shop.

The others continued to fire and were getting closer as we slowed down, stuck in traffic. Kenny jumped out of the car. Holding his gun in two hands he aimed and shot another biker.

People screamed and scattered for cover as the bullets bounced off parked cars. The sounds of sirens were getting closer as the gun battle continued. Kenny walked over to an injured biker lying in the street and fired one bullet into his helmet.

As the police got closer, the bikers retreated. We grabbed the plunder from the back seat and abandoned Kenny's car.

"Damn, I really liked that car," he said.

"Come on, there's a subway station at the corner," I shouted.

We headed back to the apartment on Tenth Avenue making sure no one tailed us. When we walked in, Jackie was there, watching TV.

"Take a walk Jackie. Go to the store and get us a carton of cigs," Kenny said.

She looked at him with pure hatred. She grabbed her keys and left, slamming the door behind her.

Kenny sat on the couch and emptied the gym bag on the table. My eyes nearly popped out of my head as he counted thirty stacks of hundred dollar bills.

"Bill, this is a lot of fucking money," he said. "We

gotta give most of this to Mr. Sullivan. It will keep him off our backs."

"What about the dope?" I asked.

"I'll get rid of that with some people I know," he said.

"If the Mexicans hated me for killing Manny, they're going to be steaming for you," I teased.

"Let me see what you found in the freezer." I handed it over to him, and he examined both bags. "A kilo of cocaine is probably worth about forty thousand dollars. This baby here is worth a whole lot more," Kenny said. He held up the bag filled with heroin. "I think it's a wash," he said.

"What do you mean?" I asked.

"This is probably worth around two hundred thousand dollars. We made a big huge haul bro. I knew they had some stuff, but this is fucking crazy."

CHAPTER SIXTEEN

The next morning I was lying in bed thinking about the whole ordeal that Kenny got me into with the drug dealers. He could easily have gotten me killed last night. I started to think there was something I'd missed. What was it?

Oh fuck! I missed my date again with Dana. Oh no, she would never accept another apology for my ditching her again. What could I do?

I picked up my phone and dialed her number. It rang, and rang, rang. After the fifth ring her voicemail picked up the call. I heard her sweet voice and my heart dropped at my stupidity. "This is Dana I can't get to the phone right now, so leave a message."

I breathed into the phone for a few beats trying to figure out what to say. "Dana, hi this is Bill, I'm sorry for standing you up again. I got stuck on an assignment at work and couldn't call you. I know you're probably pretty steamed at me, but I'm so sorry. Give me a call later… Umm, or I'll try you again soon."

I felt like crawling under the table. "You're such an asshole," I shouted. I smacked my forehead and let out a giant sigh. I flopped backwards onto my bed, listening to the bedsprings squeak. I was staring at the stucco ceiling when all of a sudden my phone started vibrating. I bolted straight up hoping it was Dana calling me back. I grabbed the phone; of course not, it was Kenny.

"Yeah," I answered.

"That's how you answer the fucking phone?" he asked.

"Oh sorry. I meant to say 'Good morning, this is Bill'," I replied.

"Cut the shit. I'm down at the curb."

"Okay, I'll be right there."

I looked at the time and saw it was already eleven o'clock. I pushed myself out of bed and went into the bathroom. I shaved, slapped on some cologne, brushed my teeth, and combed my hair. I got dressed fast then rushed out the door.

Kenny was waiting in a new grey Mercury Grand Marquis, jamming to something dark on the radio; I think it was Nine Inch Nails. He was rocking and tapping on the steering wheel. He was in a stellar mood, full of electricity in anticipation of our meeting with Mr. Sullivan.

"I bought Mr. Sullivan some new shoes. I know he'll love them," Kenny said, grinning.

"You know his size?" I asked.

"Fuck no, I don't know his size," he said, looking at me with disgust, like I ruined his moment. "It's the fucking money, you idiot."

"Do we need an appointment?" I asked.

"No, he already knows what went down. After all, he is the boss."

He pulled away from the curb, tires smoking as he floored the accelerator. When we arrived downtown, he parked around the corner in an outdoor parking lot. Kenny got out, opened the back door of the Mercury, and pulled out a Macy's shopping bag. There were three shoeboxes in the bag, all filled with money from the Mexican drug house.

Kenny looked down at the bag, and then up at me, smiling like a little kid.

"He'll love these shoes," he said.

"I hope they're his size," I added.

"Oh they'll fit. Or he can take them back," he said.

We walked around the corner and over to McKenzie's. Morgan waved us over.

"I heard you boys had a busy night and you still had time to go shopping for Mr. Sullivan. How nice," Morgan said, with a smile.

Kenny looked around. "Is Mr. Sullivan here?" he asked.

Morgan stood. "We expect him any minute," he said. "I can put that in the office for you."

"This is a very special gift and we prefer a personal touch," Kenny said, patting the side of the bag.

"Very well," he said.

We walked over to the bar, and Kenny ordered two doubles of Jameson. "I'm a little short right now," he said. "Pay for the drink." He grinned at me.

We were sipping the whiskey when Mr. Sullivan's Lincoln pulled up at the front door. Two guards came in with him, one in front, and one behind. Everyone stopped to acknowledge the boss as he walked into the room. He immediately went over to Morgan, who whispered in his ear. Mr. Sullivan nodded with his eyes locked on the bag Kenny was carrying. He went up the stairs, and Morgan came over. "Mr. Sullivan would like to speak to you about last night upstairs. Please follow me."

We finished our whiskey, and followed along. When we entered the office, Morgan closed the door behind us. Mr. Sullivan sat behind the desk and leaned forward, a pained expression on his face. He paused for several seconds, and then said, "You boys have created quite a ruckus last night. The police have nothing to go on except a bunch of dead Mexicans."

I started to say something, but Kenny cut me off. "I apologize for bringing you any additional trouble, Mr. Sullivan. I was just running a little training exercise with Bill, and wanted to show him how to be a good earner."

"I see," Mr. Sullivan said, placing his hands in a steeple over his lips. He paused in thought, eyes closed. "And how did the training work out?" he said.

Kenny handed Mr. Sullivan the bag, ginning ear to

ear. "It was a little messy, but I think you'll be pleased. If you are disappointed in any way we will stop the training."

He took the three shoeboxes out of the shopping bag and laid them on the table. He removed the lids to peek inside. A big grin grew on his face. He held out his hands, gesturing for us to come closer.

"Well done, boys. Very well done. This will send a clear message not to shoot up our clubs," he said.

Mr. Sullivan put his arm around Kenny and squeezed. He came over to me, patted my face, and pinched my cheek.

"Now listen boys, you hurt these guys enough, they're gonna come after us hard until they feel vindicated. Be very careful until this settles down."

"Okay, boss. I'll keep an eye on Bill," Kenny said.

We left the office and headed out to the street. I fired up a cig, took a drag, and blew smoke into the air. "Now what?" I said.

"We gotta sell this shit fast," Kenny said.

I tapped the cigarette, and ashes fell to the ground. "Who's gonna buy it?" I asked.

"The Russians will," he said. "Let's take a ride."

"Where are we going?" I asked.

"Brooklyn."

We drove downtown, then over the Manhattan Bridge into Brooklyn. I gazed at the water view, boats, and people strolling on the bike path. I drifted, mesmerized by the rhythm of the waves. If only I had a normal life and a normal job, I might be able to spend time with Dana and walk on the water's edge and really give her the attention she deserved. My mind saw an image of her face, smiling and looking sad from that morning after we had spent the night together. I wasn't even sure she would let me get close to her after all this bullshit. I was feeling like a real dirt bag "This is real nice," I said, trying pull myself back from my thoughts.

"Yeah, I took the scenic route. Enjoy."

Kenny exited at Coney Island Avenue and pulled up in front of a brick apartment building. He parked and we waited in the car.

Kenny reached into his jacket and pulled out his gun. He slid the mechanism back and chambered a round. "I've known these guys for a long time, they can be touchy and unpredictable. Their business is drugs, Eastern European girls, and loan sharking." He opened the door, and said, "Let's go."

"Okay," I said, and followed him.

"Dmitry's the super of this building, and a lieutenant in the local Russian mob. Let's just hope this goes well," he said.

I was nervous, and my palms were sweaty. Kenny scanned the apartment numbers and pressed apartment 1A.

A voice with a heavy Russian accent responded. "Yeah, what do you want?"

"It's Kenny Shea."

The door buzzed and Kenny pushed it open. We walked through the lobby, our shoes echoing in a combination of squeaks and taps. The door slammed behind us with a loud bang and I almost jumped out of my skin.

When we got to 1A, the door suddenly opened. A block of a man stood at the door. He scanned us up and down. "Come in, Dmitry is in the back."

In the first room six men played cards at a large rectangle table, money scattered around the edge, with a big pile in the middle. I noticed a couple of the guys wore gun holsters. Bottles, glasses, and ashtrays were everywhere. Their yelling and laughing stopped abruptly as we entered the apartment. After we passed, the game resumed, with banter in Russian and English as they played.

In the back was a small kitchen, back lit by a dirty window. Two men sat at a square table, a bottle of vodka and shot glasses in the middle. As Kenny approached, one guy stood up and gave him a big hug. He was tall, with bushy black hair and a full beard.

In a thick Russian accent, he said, "It's so good to see you, my friend. Remember Viktor."

Viktor got up and shook hands with Kenny.

"Sure, it's been a while, but I remember."

Viktor had a shaved head, black goatee, and bulging muscles. Dmitry poured a shot and drank, knocking it back fast. "Who is this?" he asked.

"This is Bill, my new partner," Kenny replied.

"Sit, and drink with us."

We pulled out the chairs and sat at the table. Viktor put two more shot glasses on the table and Dmitry filled them. Dmitry held up his glass. "*Za Vas!* And now, down with the business."

Kenny took out the two bags, one white and the

other dark brown. "Feel free to test it if you like," he said.

Dmitry said something in Russian to Viktor. He left the room and came back with a black leather pouch. Viktor pulled out a knife, cut open the bag, and began testing the heroin. Dmitry seemed excited and focused on the white bag in front of him. He opened a drawer, pulled out scissors, and cut the bag. He licked the side of the scissor, and said, "Uh huh." Then he tapped a little onto a mirror and chopped at it with a credit card. He snorted it through a rolled up hundred dollar bill, sniffed a few times, and wiped his nose.

"You know, Kenny, I have plenty of this stuff. I'll take it off your hands, but it's gotta be worth it," he said, smiling.

"Okay, let's see when Viktor is done testing."

Viktor leaned over and whispered into Dmitry's ear. Dmitry looked at us. "The coke is good, nothing special, but black tar heroin is a different story. Top shelf stuff. I'll give you one twenty-five for both," he said.

"Wow, you're really cutting down my profit. Two hundred or it's not worth the trouble."

"Okay, be fair. You make some, I make some. Let's meet in the middle, one fifty." Dmitry said.

"I can't do it. Come on, you can get double on the street," Kenny pleaded.

"There is truth in that. I'll tell you what, one seventy-five. I'll even throw in this fine bottle of vodka," he said.

"I'll accept your offer only if we drink on it," Kenny offered.

Dmitry spoke Russian again to Viktor, and he left the room. After a few minutes he came back with a brown paper bag, and laid it down.

"Hey Bill, is this your first deal?" he asked.

"Yeah, first drug deal," I replied.

"Kenny, you check the bag, and then we drink," Dmitry said.

Kenny picked up the bag, took the money out, and stacked it on the table. The three of us watched as Kenny counted it, and put it back in the bag.

"Let's drink," Kenny said.

We drank, smoked, and laughed. They were very likable. I couldn't figure out why Kenny said they were touchy, but we still hadn't made it out alive with the money.

After we finished the bottle that was on the table, Dmitry pulled out another bottle. Kenny stood up. "Okay, my friend, it's time for us to go. Any more drinking and the cops will pick us up on the way home," he said.

Dmitry opened the new bottle and poured another round.

Kenny stood up and knocked back his glass. "Thanks for the business," Kenny said, and picked up the bag. Viktor grabbed his hand, then said something to Dmitry in Russian. It had an angry tone. Dmitry replied in Russian, agitated.

"I'm sorry about this, Kenny. Give me a few minutes to speak to Viktor."

They both got up and went into another room off the kitchen, closing the door. Suddenly we heard some loud shouting. I looked at Kenny and he put a finger to his lips. Dmitry returned alone.

"Let's go now, and I will walk you to your car. There are some bad folks in this area, and we wouldn't want any trouble."

As we walked by the poker game, silence filled the

room. All eyes were on the brown paper bag Kenny carried. Viktor came out of the back room and whispered into one guy's ear. He put his hand on a gun that was sitting on the table next to him.

I could feel sweat dripping down my back. This must be the touchy part Kenny spoke of. We could've been blown away at any time.

Dmitry turned to Viktor, and said something low under his breath. They all stood still, eyes darted from one another. The tension was thick.

We slowly made our way out of the apartment and into the corridor, with Dmitry behind us. He rushed us to the car, practically pushing me the whole way. Even Dmitry seemed nervous. He brushed sweat from his brow. "We've been having a power struggle in the group. Unfortunately this deal may get the whole ball rolling. I may have to... um. How do you say? Um... nip this in the bud. You call me in a couple of weeks, Kenny. Okay?"

"Okay, Dmitry. Good luck."

CHAPTER SEVENTEEN

We didn't say a word on the way back from Brooklyn. When we finally crossed the Manhattan Bridge I asked, "Are they always that uptight?"

"Yeah, the Russians are always breaking off into their small crews. Sometimes it works out, and they get along. Other times bodies start washing up. I told you they were a touchy bunch."

"Man! You were right, that was scary. One second everything was all friendly, the next they were ready for war," I said.

"Let's go over to my place and split up the cash," he said.

Kenny's apartment was in the west 60s by Central Park. In a lot of ways it was similar to where I was living. It had a doorman and a reception desk, but no one else was living with him. "Where's your girl?" I asked.

"Got rid of her," he said. "I don't need anyone

reporting back to Sullivan about what I'm doing."

"I had no idea that's why Jackie was there," I said.

"Why else would Sullivan give you an awesome apartment with your own Geisha?"

Kenny's apartment was on the tenth floor. It had modern furniture and stainless steel appliances. Tall windows overlooked the Park. I walked over to the windows and took in the view.

Kenny came out of a back room with a shoebox and the brown paper bag. He dumped the cash out on the coffee table. After he finished counting, it turned out to be two hundred and seventy-five thousand dollars. I thought I was dreaming.

Kenny split the left over money from the drug bust, and what we received from the Russians. He put half the cash in the brown bag. Then he leaned back on the couch and fired up a cig. "This is a nice big haul for you, Bill. You'd better not go crazy spending it, and don't let Jackie know, or she'll report you to Sullivan. Rudy made that mistake, and you saw what Whelan did to him, poor guy."

I nodded.

"I always give Sullivan big money. If Sullivan

found out about my split I'd end up strapped to a chair in the basement. There's no way I could pull this off without contact with rival gangs. Don't think it was me that put Rudy in that position. He shot off his mouth way too much with that chick in the apartment. The only difference is I don't sell info about Sullivan's organization. Rudy became too friendly with Dmitry and started leaking.

He finished his cig and looked me in the eye. "Take your money and be smart. If I were you I'd kick Jackie out as soon as you can. She'll turn you in to Whelan and you'll be meatloaf for pigs upstate on his farm."

Now I lit up a cig, blew out the smoke, and then said, "Thanks Kenny, this is incredible. I had you figured all wrong I guess."

"Just be careful, and keep an eye on her," Kenny said.

I left his apartment, my head spinning. I couldn't figure out who was telling the truth. Time would tell. I only hoped to make the right choice at the right time.

On my way home, I couldn't stop thinking about what Kenny had said. Was Jackie really reporting my activities? Did Rudy really have a cozy connection with the Russians? I had to find out what happened. Something went wrong and Kenny sacrificed Rudy to cover his tracks. Or was it Jackie? I wondered if Mr. Sullivan knew Kenny was still dealing with the Russians. It was a dangerous game and I was getting deeper in it with every move.

Things were quiet for the next few days. I went back to my old apartment in Hell's Kitchen. I couldn't go back to Jackie and the other apartment until I cleared my head. Dana didn't call me, she must've been so pissed off, so I called her and left another message. This time I apologized and offered to make it up to her if she'd just call me back. I didn't hear from Kenny during that time. I thought he must've been lining things up for the next big haul.

I drank, read, and visited Jimmy. He was doing very well. The doctors were cutting back on his medicine. He was still excited about his new love Tracy. They were helping each other one day at a time. Jimmy and Tracy had quickly become best friends. I'd never seen Jimmy so happy or interested in a woman like this before. I was glad for him and Tracy, but sad for Dana and me. I'd fucked things up royally and all I could do was drink the pain away.

I decided to call up Dana late one night after a few shots of bourbon. I dialed Dana's number and she answered on the first ring.

"You have some nerve calling me, stop leaving messages and go bother someone else who doesn't care if you stand them up all the time," she said. Her voice was angry, but still had that sweet twang with a sassy southern drawl.

"I'm sorry, Dana. I've had a bunch of problems and I didn't want to expose you to it. Bad people were after me, and I thought you might get hurt."

"I've seen your kind before, Bill. You're a user. You only come around when it suits you," she said.

"Dana, I really care for you. I'll make it up to you. Please give me a chance."

The silence was deafening, but she didn't hang up. I could hear her breathing.

"Fuck you. Bill, I'm done with your crap."

"Dana, please meet me. I need to see you, and I'll explain." I said, but the phone was dead.

Later that night I picked up the Lincoln from the

garage and headed over to Dana's apartment. I knew I needed to discuss my situation with Dana and she would never agree to meet me. I hoped she'd still be interested in me after she understood my job. I would do my best to beg her forgiveness and explain the truth about this crazy mess I was in.

I parked the Lincoln on a side street and walked over to Dana's place. I pressed her apartment buzzer and waited. I thought she would say something through the intercom, but she just buzzed me in. I made a mental note to tell her to be more careful.

I went up the stairs and knocked on the door. When Dana didn't answer, I tried the doorknob and found it was unlocked. I walked into the apartment and something hit me. A white flash of pain exploded in my head, blinding me as darkness engulfed me.

I had a hard time recognizing where I was. I was strapped to a chair. My arms and legs were immobilized. I looked around the room, and all was dark except for one light bulb hanging over my seat. The pain behind my eyes still throbbed and the back of my skull ached, which made me nauseated again. I tried to focus on the room, but couldn't focus or see beyond the lighted area surrounding my confinement.

I sat there for a while. It could've been a few minutes or a few hours. At one point I blacked out again. When I awoke there was vomit on my shirt and lap. The stench made me gag.

Sometime later, a door opened behind me then slammed, echoing within the room and right through my aching head. I squeezed my eyes tight to push away the pain. Someone walked around the edge of the darkness, but I couldn't see who it was.

A deep male voice growled. "You have a sweet, beautiful girlfriend. Don't you think it would be shame if something happened to her?"

I recognized the accent immediately. It was Russian.

"You fucking touch her and I'll kill you!" I shouted.

"You have something that belongs to me. I want it back or your girlfriend will be working at our club," he said. He took a few steps out of the shadows, and walked into the light. It was Viktor, shaved head, goatee, with corded muscles bulging under his clothes. He paced, back and forth. "You and your friend made me look ridiculous. The Bratva will not be robbed by your overpriced garbage. It's an insult to our honor."

His phone went off. He reached into his jacket and answered. Yelling in Russian, he clearly wasn't happy with the person on the call. He closed the phone, looked at me. "Your friends are trying to interrupt us."

His phone went off again, he looked to see who it was, then turned it off. "Tell me where the money is."

"I don't know what your problem is, but Dmitry paid us so you should take it up with him."

He took off his jacket and hung it on a hook in the shadows. "You ripped us off. That price was ridiculous."

"Alright, so you want a refund?" I asked.

"Half the money is what I want," he answered.

"I don't have it."

He launched two fast punches. My head rocked back. Blood trickled from a cut over my right eye.

"No more bullshit." Viktor said, and picked up a long pipe off the floor.

I wasn't going to tell him anything. The more he tried, the more frustrated he became. After he started, I passed out again. I drifted in and out of consciousness. At one point I could feel the impact, but I was barely able to open my eyes. I thought I saw other people in the room, but couldn't be sure. They appeared to be dancing, but I heard no music. Viktor came closer, he screamed and spit with rage. The last thing I remember was his twisted face; inches from mine, shouting as someone pulled him away. Dark shadows closed in around me as I fell into complete darkness and silence.

CHAPTER EIGHTEEN

I heard a female voice. "Can you hear me, Mr. Conlin?"

I tried to speak, but couldn't get my mouth to form words. My voice came out in a series of mumbles. I knew what I wanted to say, but my body wouldn't cooperate.

I opened my eyes. Looking around, it appeared I was in the hospital or something. I looked at the woman, who had spoken to me, a nurse, as she adjusted an intravenous drip hanging on my right side. "Are you in any pain? Just nod, or make a sound, if you can."

I nodded.

"I'll get you something for your pain."

Moments later she returned and injected

something into my IV. The pain subsided, and I faded out.

For what seemed like weeks, I was kept medicated, then began to regain my strength. One day a doctor came by to visit while I was awake. I struggled to speak to him, but I couldn't.

"Just take it easy," he said. "You've come a long way in a short time. Your jaw's been wired shut to help it heal."

"What happened?" I asked through clenched teeth.

He wrote some notes on my chart, then said, "We don't know what happened to you, but what we do know is your jaw, nose, right cheekbone, and both legs were broken in several places."

"Where's the girl? Where is Dana?" Of course he had no idea what I was talking about.

A few days later, they wheeled me to the outside patio. The sun was so bright I could barely see and squinted until my eyes adjusted. Jimmy sat at a table smoking and stood up when he saw me. He put out his cigarette in an ashtray, came over and gave me a hug.

"Bill, I'm so glad to see you're doing better."

"It's good to see you, Jimmy."

"How's your physical therapy coming? I heard they are gonna be taking out the pins from your legs soon."

"Good," I said.

Jimmy was the only person to visit me regularly while I was in rehab. I was proud of him, back on track. He brought me crime novels, and picked me up for day trips to the park.

After several months I was finally feeling strong enough to leave the rehab center, but Jimmy still couldn't tell me about Dana.

"It's a long story" he said when I asked him again. "After Viktor worked you over, Kenny was able to get Dmitry to track down your location and rescue you. When they got there, you were a bloody mess and Viktor was out of his mind with rage. He was so frustrated with the lack of information that he turned his anger on Dmitry. An internal turf war broke out and the Brooklyn Russian Bratva split in two. Dmitry had a stronger position with his connections to the Irish and Italian mob. That didn't stop Viktor from robbing bagmen and busting up whorehouses.

Currently there's a price on his head. He's gone into hiding.

"But where's Dana?" I asked again.

"Kenny talked Dmitry into recovering Dana from a Russian whorehouse in Brooklyn, but before they arrived she was moved to an unknown location. Viktor is keeping her close, as his last card. We're still trying to find out where she is. I'm so sorry Bill."

"Is she alive?" I asked.

"Dmitry believes she is. Viktor is refusing to turn her over without payment of one hundred thousand dollars. It's been months since this all went down though..."

He trailed off. I sobbed with grief, my face buried in my hands. "If only I stayed away from Dana. I knew it was dangerous, but I didn't think anyone was following me. I can't believe Viktor singled me out."

Jimmy put his arm around me. "I can't imagine what you're going through, but I'll help any way I can. You've always been like a brother to me and I'm here for you now."

"Thanks Jimmy."

"I'm clean now, thanks to you. I'm married and

Mr. Sullivan took me back. I've been helping with collections again," he said.

I squeezed my fists tight, nails biting into my palms. "I gotta get out of here," I said. "I'm gonna find Dana and kill Viktor. He'll suffer, slow and painful."

"Okay Bill, take it easy. You just need to get strong and back on your feet. I'll keep my ears open, and I know Kenny is looking for Dana, too. We'll find both of them soon."

"I have the money. Contact Viktor and get proof of life. We need to make a trade immediately," I said frantically.

"How do you have that kind of money Bill?" Jimmy asked with a skeptical expression.

"I have money from ripping off some Mexican drug dealers," I answered.

I paused and took a few breaths before continuing. "Tell Kenny to make arrangements to pay Viktor. I'll trade the money for Dana, but hurry. This has gone on long enough."

"We need to speak to Mr. Sullivan before we do anything," Jimmy said.

My last day at rehab, Jimmy and Kenny came to

pick me up. Kenny climbed out of the driver's side, gave me a hug and a smack on the back. "I'm sorry about all this, but it's good to see you, Bill. Now let's go get your girl."

"Okay, but I'm not so sure I'm ready," I said, rubbing my legs.

Kenny drove uptown. "Mr. Sullivan wants to speak with you about the Russians," he said.

"Sure, I'm ready to get down to business," I replied.

Kenny pulled up in front of McKenzie's. "We'll be here when you come out," Kenny said.

I opened the car door, moved my legs to the side, and climbed out of the back seat. I planted my feet on the ground, and then used the cane to steady myself as I lifted my butt off the seat. It took a while for me to get out. The ride had made me a little stiff, but once standing I was able to straighten up and start moving.

I walked into the restaurant and stood by the door until Morgan came over, smiling, his hands held out wide. I could smell his Polo Cologne before he even got close.

He patted me on the back. "We're all glad you're

okay, Bill. Mr. Sullivan has asked me to personally help you with your problems," he said.

"Where do we start?" I asked.

"Dmitry is our main contact with the Russians. You'll go with Kenny and Jimmy, find out what he knows and report back to me." He paused, and then continued, "The apartment, car, and Jackie are all still available for you."

"Please thank Mr. Sullivan. I really appreciate all his help, but I don't want to share the apartment with Jackie anymore," I said.

"I'll pass that message onto Mr. Sullivan. For now let's just leave things as they are. Start gathering information and see how you feel."

I knew they wouldn't let me change the arrangement. They needed Jackie to get information about my activities.

Morgan moved closer and whispered in my ear. "We're working to find Viktor. Hang tight and once we are sure of his location we'll settle the score."

I could feel the rage building deep inside me. Clenching my jaw, I felt a sharp pain run along the right side of my face. The pain brought me back to reality and I needed to lighten up before I injured myself or did something stupid.

I turned to Morgan, then whispered, "Someone set me up and told Viktor where my girlfriend lived. Whoever that person is will pay with their life."

He looked at me, and said, "Just make sure you ask permission. Unsanctioned hits are extremely frowned upon."

"I understand," I said.

"Remember that we have rules that must be followed. If there is something you're not telling us, now would be a good time" he said.

"I can only hope that when I do find him I'll have time to ask permission."

"Make sure that you do," Morgan said.

As I turned to leave, pandemonium took over the bar. Word came that Mr. Sullivan's car had been ambushed in the Midtown Tunnel by a group of motorcycle assassins. His driver and bodyguards were dead at the scene, but there were rumors that the boss was still breathing.

Mr. Sullivan had been taken directly to New York Presbyterian Hospital. No other information about his condition was available. Meanwhile, the police had closed the tunnel to investigate.

The atmosphere quickly changed over to a stampede as half the men in the restaurant rushed out, their voices loud and agitated. Morgan and five men raced out to Mr. Sullivan's side to protect him from further attempts on his life.

CHAPTER NINETEEN

I walked out into the street and took a deep breath. Jimmy rolled down the window. "What's going on?"

"Someone just hit Sullivan in the Midtown Tunnel."

"Come on, get in. We have to go," Jimmy said.

Kenny leaned down to peer at me past the roofline. "Get in, let's go," he said.

I climbed in slow and carefully. "Where are we going?" I asked.

"To meet Dmitry. We have things to discuss. Morgan will take care of Mr. Sullivan," Kenny said.

As we drove, I thought about the assassination attempt, and how it had to be the Mexicans. Guys on bikes had tried to kill me the same way. The Mexicans were launching an all out war over Manny's murder and losses would be heavy on both sides.

Sullivan underestimated the Mexicans' ability to catch up with him. Angel wouldn't stop until her blood lust was satisfied. I wasn't sure she had given up on trying to kill me either. I needed to get healthy fast and walking around with a cane made me an easy target. "Hey Kenny, let's go by my apartment on 51st before we head over to Brooklyn. I need to pick up a few things."

"Just make it fast." Kenny said.

Kenny pulled the Mercury Grand Marquis in front of the building. I climbed out of the back seat and hobbled to the front door. The doorman held the door open for me.

"Welcome back, sir. I'm glad to see you well again."

Thanks, Tony. It's good to be back," I said.

While waiting for the elevator I started to think back before the beating. I left all the cash in the apartment upstairs. Could it still be there after so long being out of commission? I was about to find out.

I used the cane as I made my way down the

hallway to the apartment and knocked on the door. A few seconds passed, then the door opened. Jackie smiled at me. "Welcome home. I hope you're feeling better."

"Yes, I'm getting there. Slow, but steady."

"Well, are you coming in?" she asked.

"Yes, just for a quick sec."

I stepped in and Jackie closed the door behind me. I went straight into the bedroom and unlocked the armoire. On the left, rifles and shotguns hung on hooks. I opened the first drawer, grabbed a Beretta and loaded the clip. I pulled out the middle drawer and gazed at all different size combat knives. I took two Browning compact push daggers and put one in each pocket. The money I left in the armoire from my deals with Kenny was untouched.

I came out of the bedroom and Jackie was sitting on the couch watching TV, a drink in her hand. She put the drink down and walked toward me. I moved towards the front door.

"I like your beard. It looks good. How are you feeling?" she asked, looking from my face down to my legs.

"I'm getting stronger every day," I replied.

"Well, I'm glad you made it out alive," she said, without emotion.

"Thanks, I'll be back later," I said.

"I'll be here."

I closed the apartment door and went down in the elevator, walked through the lobby and out into the street.

I climbed into the back seat of Kenny's car.

"Hey what happened to all my stuff at my old apartment?"

Kenny turned around.

"What kind of friend would I be if we didn't take care of your stuff? I paid your rent and kept your apartment going for you."

"Thanks Kenny. I thought for sure the landlord had taken all my stuff by now."

"Are you kidding, Bill? We take care of our own." Kenny smiled, turned forward, glanced at his side mirror, and pulled away from the curb.

About forty minutes later we arrived at Dmitry's building. When we got out of Kenny's car, five large men immediately intercepted us. They came out of parked cars guns drawn.

"You won't need this," one guy said, and took Kenny's gun from inside his jacket. Jimmy and I were also stripped of our guns. The big Russians roughed us up a bit.

"Hey, take it easy. We're here to speak to Dmitry," Jimmy said, getting shoved against the car.

"He's expecting us. Just check with him," I said, a little rattled by the treatment.

The lead guy was built solid and tall, with a heavy accent. He took out a phone, pressed a button, and waited. After a few seconds he started speaking Russian in short low bursts of words. He turned back to us. "Which one of you is Kenny?" he asked.

"I am," Kenny replied.

"Here take this. Someone wants to talk," he said.

Kenny held the phone up to his ear. "Hello?" Kenny listened for a few seconds. "I understand. Not a problem, yes I understand."

Kenny handed the phone back to the large man. He turned to the other men, spoke in Russian, and they handed us our weapons. "You are free to go." He said.

"Let's get back in the car," Kenny said.

"What? We're not even finished?" I said aggravated.

"Sorry Bill, get in the car." Kenny said.

I climbed back into Kenny's car. He slowly pulled away from the curb and made a U-turn.

"What's going on?" I asked.

"Things are too hot for Dmitry to meet us at his place. Just hold on Bill." He answered.

We drove for a few minutes and parked near a strip of local stores. On the other side of the street were brick apartment buildings. Kenny opened his door and stepped out. He walked around to my side, opened the door. "Come on, let's get something to eat," he said.

We went into a small Russian café. A sweet and sour aroma of beet soup, brisket, and fried onions immediately made me hungry. A waitress greeted us with a smile. "Sit anywhere you like," she said, with a slight Russian accent.

She was attractive, with blonde streaked hair tied in a ponytail. She wore a white button-down blouse and black pants with a dark red apron.

All the tables and chairs were made of dark wood.

A couple of tables had customers eating and speaking Russian. Most of the restaurant was empty, and we sat in the back and waited.

The waitress approached, handed us menus, then took out a pad and pen from her apron. "Would you like something to drink?"

"We're waiting for someone. Please give us a few minutes," Kenny said, smiling as he looked up from his menu.

"Okay, I'll bring you water while you decide," she said, and walked off.

I leaned over across the table. "What are we doing here?"

"We are waiting for a call from Dmitry. It is too dangerous to meet in known hot spots. Things have gotten heated," he explained.

The waitress came back with four glasses of water on a tray. The glasses were filled with ice that clinked as she served us. We waited for twenty minutes. I was ready to order something, but Kenny wasn't sure we were staying.

I looked around and noticed that the restaurant was empty, and that the front door had been closed.

Four large men walked in and waited at the front. They looked familiar, and then I recognized the lead guy from Dmitry's apartment building. He came over to Kenny, whispered in his ear, and sat at a table opposite us.

After a while Dmitry came in. He walked straight into the back and joined us. He waved the waitress over and ordered several dishes in Russian. "This is a mess. All this tension and violence is not good for business," he said.

The waitress came back with four shot glasses and a bottle of vodka. Dmitry poured the vodka, and said, "*Pei do dna!*" He knocked back the shot and poured another.

"What does that mean?" I asked.

"It means, drink to the bottom," he answered.

We did several rounds.

"I'm sorry things turned so ugly, Bill. This is not the way I do business. These youngsters have no honor or respect for old relationships," Dmitry said low, putting his hand on my arm.

"Where are Viktor and the girl?" I asked, pulling my arm away.

"I understand your concern, Bill. This is a little complicated. I will make things right and we will get the girl back. Viktor won't hurt her cause he wants your money."

Dmitry poured a shot and drank it fast, then poured another. "We know where Viktor is, but he has many men with him day and night. The girl is in another location and it's well guarded," Dmitry said.

"Give us the address and we'll deal with whoever is guarding Dana," I said.

"It's not that easy. Mikhail will go with you as my representative," he said, holding out his left hand to the guy sitting at the other table.

"You trust this guy?" I asked.

"Da, I trust Mikhail with my life. He is one of my best men." I looked over to Mikhail. His eyes were locked on me, and his face was stone, with no expression.

"If you need to speak to anyone, Mikhail can translate. He also knows this location very well. It's a whorehouse in Queens that we use to run before the split," Dmitry said.

"Where is this place?" I asked.

"Forest Hills, off Yellowstone Boulevard."

"Where is Viktor?" I asked.

"Kenny and I will deal with Viktor," he said.

"Not without me. I want Viktor alive. I promised Morgan."

"Not to worry, you get the girl with Mikhail. That is the plan," he said.

"This is bullshit. Who made this fucked up plan?" I asked.

"Kenny did," he replied.

I stared at Kenny and he smiled back at me with his sleepy eyes. "Why were we splitting up? Dmitry and Kenny going off to get Viktor didn't feel right. I didn't like how this was shaping up." I thought.

"What are you gonna do with Viktor if you can grab him?" I asked.

"Kenny will bring him to you as a gift from me. I want peace more than anyone. I taught Viktor everything he knows. It's only fair that I bring him down," Dmitry answered, and then he did another shot.

"Okay, but Jimmy is with me."

Dmitry turned to Mikhail, and asked, "Is that a

problem?"

"Nyet."

"Okay, that will be fine, and we have our plan," Dmitry said.

The waitress returned with the food. After several trips and help from another waiter, the table was filled with delicious food. The aroma was incredible. She brought out beef stroganoff and chicken stew, breaded schnitzel with egg and lamb kebabs, assorted vegetables and beet soup. I couldn't decide where to start. The table was so maxed out that we combined tables with Mikhail.

"Eat and enjoy my friends. Now we put an end to our problems," Dmitry said, holding up his shot glass and knocking back more vodka.

CHAPTER TWENTY

After we finished eating, Dmitry asked us to follow him out to his car. He climbed into the passenger side and took out his cell phone. A few seconds later he spoke to the person on the other end in Russian. Whatever they said became heated; he ended the call, sighed and shook his head.

"He waved me to come closer.

"What's going on?" I asked, walking over to the car and placing my hands on the roof and the open door.

"I called Viktor. Now we wait for a call back with your proof of life. It shouldn't be too long," he explained.

I fired up a cig, took a deep drag and blew out the smoke. Leaning against the car and tried to act patient, but I wasn't fooling anyone. Kenny and Jimmy both looked at me and shrugged. We all looked to Mikhail. His face wasn't giving anything away as he stared back at us with the same stone expression.

Jimmy started pacing, and chain smoking. He really was getting on my nerves.

"Jimmy, be a pal. Go up the block and get us some beer at that deli," I said.

"Good idea," he said, then nodded and walked off. A few minutes later he returned with the beer, and handed them out. Mikhail refused the offer with a shake of his head. Time slowed to a crawl. I could feel myself aging years from the stress of waiting.

An hour passed and still nothing happened. No call and no text message. "Exactly what proof are we waiting for Dmitry?" I asked.

He held one finger up to his lips. "Shush." It was long and slow.

I closed my eyes and took a big breath, exhaling slowly. I wiped sweat from my forehead and looked at Jimmy. He shrugged his shoulders, and took a deep drag of his cigarette.

Suddenly Dmitry's phone began buzzing.

Everyone stared at him as he answered it. He said a few words in Russian, but this time there was no argument from the other side.

"Da, da." Then he handed me the phone. "Go ahead Bill. This is what you've been waiting for."

I held the phone to my ear. "Hello?"

I heard a women crying on the other end. "Dana, its Bill. Are you okay? I know it's been a long time, but I'm gonna get you out of this. Just hold tight," I said.

I heard a women scream, but couldn't tell if it was Dana. A deep male voice came on the phone speaking Russian. I handed the phone back to Dmitry and he started arguing with the guy on the phone and ended the call.

Dmitry's phone buzzed once. He looked at it for a few seconds and then gave it to me again. A picture of Dana was on the phone.

"How the fuck do I know if she's alive from that picture? I asked, irritated.

Dmitry took the phone from my hand. "Now you have proof of life.

"What? That's shit!" I barked.

It's all the proof you're getting. Victor told me any

more games and she's dead. Give the money to Kenny, and then we meet with Viktor. You, Jimmy, and Mikhail go get the girl. When we hand over the money to Viktor she will be released to you. I'll make sure to call you, before we walk away."

"This deal stinks, Kenny. I want Viktor alive when this is over," I demanded.

"We'll grab him if we can, but no promises. It all depends what kind of muscle he has with him when we meet," Dmitry said.

On the way back, I stared out the window as we crossed the Manhattan Bridge. I couldn't help but wonder if this was a dirty deal. Kenny had been unpredictable on many occasions, but in my favor. "Kenny, please tell me this is not one of your fucked up double crosses?"

"No worries, Bill. I have this all under control," he replied.

"I still feel like there's something you're not telling me," I said.

Kenny adjusted his rearview mirror so he could see my face. "Just give me the money and have a little faith. You might be surprised at the outcome."

We arrived at my apartment on Tenth Avenue and I headed up to get the money. I brought it down, got into the back seat, and handed it over to Kenny.

"Wow, kid! It's still in the brown paper bag I gave you," Kenny said, as he looked in the bag.

Kenny took out his cell phone and called Dmitry. "Where do you want to meet? Yes I have the money. Okay, see you there."

We drove back to Brooklyn and met with the Russians. This time it was at a different restaurant about a mile away from the earlier café. We didn't go in. "You go with Mikhail and we will meet Viktor with a few of the boys. Kenny will call you when things are set on our end," Dmitry said.

"It's five thirty. If you don't hear from us by nine there's a problem and we meet back here," Kenny said.

"Tell me where you guys are meeting Viktor," I said. "If something bad goes down I want to know where to find the bodies."

"Mikhail knows what to do if things go wrong," Dmitry said.

We drove to Forest Hills in Mikhail's van. It was an old, beat up white electrician's van. A red sign on the side of the van read "Duffy's Electrical Contractors." Metal tool cases with drawers lined the inside walls. Extension cords, PVC pipes of all sizes, drills and a large toolbox, filled the back. The side and back windows were covered for privacy.

We parked on the side of a red brick building at 63rd Drive, then watched and waited for the phone call. A side entrance with a ramp went down to a lower level. It seemed like a very busy place. Men were coming and going every few minutes.

Fifteen minutes, thirty minutes, an hour, all went by excruciatingly slowly. Over ninety minutes had passed, and I began to feel anxious, the tension making my stomach ache. Eight o'clock came and went, and Jimmy started pounding his hand on the floor of the van in frustration.

"What the fuck is taking so long?" he snapped.

"We wait, just like Dmitry said," Mikhail replied.

Time seemed to stop. Seconds passed like hours and a stress fever started burning my ears, my head beginning to pound with a head ache. I chain smoked until I was out, without even realizing it.

"This is bullshit, let's go," I said, agitated.

"We wait until nine as agreed," Mikhail said, looking at his watch.

I looked at Jimmy bouncing his leg and tapping his foot without rest.

"Let's fucking go," Jimmy said.

I scratched at the stubble on my face. Mikhail was calm and expressionless.

"This is shaving years off my life," I said, trying to contain myself. I could feel seconds ticking by at a crawl. "Something must've gone wrong. This is taking too long," I said.

"Yeah, this is real bad," Jimmy chimed in.

At eight forty-five Mikhail's phone started buzzing. He answered it and spoke in Russian. After a few short sentences he ended the call and opened the door.

"It is time to go," he said.

"What did they say? What happened?" I asked.

He didn't reply and walked around to the back of the van, opening the back doors. He climbed in and took keys out of his pocket. Mikhail unlocked a metal toolbox on the floor, took out a shotgun and shells.

As he loaded shells into the shotgun, I asked, "Did

everything go well? Are we getting Dana now?"

Mikhail didn't look up, but kept loading shells into the side. "Nyet."

"No?" I asked, shocked.

"We go in now," he said.

"What happened?" I demanded.

"Kenny will tell you later. We have some work to do," he said.

Jimmy and I got out of the van and followed Mikhail through the side entrance of the building. We went down the ramp and came to an unlocked metal door. Inside was a dimly lit hallway with tile floor. Mikhail marched down to a door at the end of the hallway and banged on it with the side of his fist. We heard a voice inside yelling in Russian and Mikhail replied. To my surprise the door unlocked and Mikhail went in. He peeked back out at us and waved us in. I took out my gun and put my other hand in my pocket. Jimmy had his gun out too as we entered the apartment.

Inside the apartment, a few girls sat on a couch watching TV. They glanced at us as we passed, then turned their faces back to the show. We went into a back room to find Viktor sitting at a table with a big smile on his face. He looked different, his hair grown out, black, wavy, and greased back.

"You don't look to be in such bad shape after our session, Bill," Viktor said, as he puffed on a cigar and blew out a big cloud of smoke. "I will have my money now and tell you where to get the girl."

Mikhail was standing on my left and said something in Russian to Viktor. I could see Viktor's face change as rage swelled inside him. "You want to fuck me, after all this time," he hissed.

"Dmitry and Kenny have the money," I explained.

Viktor spat in my face. "You're dead and so is your girl. I want that money now," he barked.

Viktor pulled out a pistol from behind his back and put it on the table. Mikhail spoke to him again and he looked at me.

Suddenly Viktor's phone rang, and he answered it, growling low in Russian. After being interrupted each time he began to speak, Viktor exploded. He screamed into the phone and threw it across the room. It shattered against the wall and broke into pieces, which rained down to the floor. Silence filled the room, and the only sound was Viktor's panting.

"Your friends have fucked us both. They want to split the money with me for your life."

"What?" I said. I heard Mikhail pump his shotgun and he pressed it against my back.

Jimmy was standing in the doorway and looked in. "What's going on in there? Are you okay Bill?" Jimmy asked.

"There's a problem with the deal," I said.

"What problem?" he asked, starting to panic.

"Dmitry and Kenny cut their own deal," I answered.

"Sorry Bill, we have other plans for you," Mikhail said.

CHAPTER TWENTY-ONE

Mikhail shoved the shotgun hard into my back.

"There's something you should know before this goes any further," I said.

"What are you saying?" Viktor said, through a clenched jaw. I slowly took my hand out of my pocket. "In case you don't recognize this, it's a grenade with the pin pulled. Make a move and we all die," I warned.

Viktor's eyes darted to Mikhail and back to me. He was trying to will Mikhail to do something with his eyes, but Mikhail didn't want to die this way.

"Mikhail, go stand by Viktor. Put your shotgun and keys on the table," I snarled.

Jimmy came into the room. No one moved for several breaths.

"Do it now!" I screamed.

"Whoa, what gives Bill?" Jimmy asked, peeking into the kitchen.

"These fuckers were gonna keep the money and kill us. It's another one of Kenny's twisted games," I said.

"That's fucking crazy. Why would they do that?" Jimmy asked.

"Cause Kenny's a crazy money hungry bastard," I replied.

"Take the keys and the shotgun and go start the van. We're going for a little ride."

"Okay, Bill" he said.

"Let's go guys," I said.

"We're not going anywhere with you asshole," Viktor shouted.

I walked over, tossed the table and shot him in the knee. He howled in pain, as blood soaked his pants. He lay on the floor clutching his injured leg, and rocked in pain, grunting.

The girls in the living room started screaming to Viktor in Russian, but he was unable to answer. I heard the front door slam as one girl ran out into the hallway screeching with fear. Our time here was at an end and we had to leave fast.

"You're a dead man! A dead man!" Viktor bellowed.

Mikhail backed up against the wall without making a sound. I pointed the gun at his face. "You carry Viktor out to the van." When he didn't move, I yelled, "Pick him up now or I'll put a fucking hole in your face."

Mikhail put his arm under Viktor and around his back and lifted him off the floor. They slowly walked towards the door while I followed behind, grenade still in hand.

"If you're thinking about getting stupid, remember, I drop this we all die," I reminded them.

The girls in the living room screamed and pressed themselves against the far wall. Two girls began crying and holding onto each other. We walked out of the apartment and into the dark hallway. I stayed a few steps behind as Mikhail dragged Viktor out of the building. Mikhail stopped every few yards to get a better grip on Viktor. As we came out Jimmy jumped out of the driver's door.

"Wow, he's bleeding a lot," he said, nervously.

"Open the back of the van, quickly."

Jimmy went to the back of the van and opened both doors. I told them to get in, and ordered Mikhail to tie Viktor's hands behind his back using some wire that was in the van. He paused to look around and I jabbed him in the back of the head with the nose of the gun.

"Now tie his ankles."

"Jimmy, come tie up Mikhail. Hurry the fuck up," I barked.

He tied Mikhail's hands behind his back and wrapped the wire around his ankles.

I climbed into the back of the van and bent over Viktor. "Where is the girl?"

He was barely conscious, but still managed to say, "Fuck you!"

I smacked him with the bottom of the pistol and he immediately passed out.

"Okay Mikhail, it's your turn. Where's the girl?"

He spat in my face. I raised the gun to hit him then stopped. He closed his eyes tight, anticipating the coming blow. I took hold of two of his fingers and pulled them back. The tension released with a snap as bones broke like dry tree branches. He screamed in pain.

"Where is the girl?" I asked again.

He shouted at me in Russian, spittle dripping onto the van floor. I held another finger. "Still not ready, aye?"

"I don't know, please don't," he pleaded.

Again I pulled his finger back until I heard the crack. He grunted and panted, breathing hard while trying to suppress the pain.

"I'm gonna brake every finger until you tell me, fucker," I hissed.

"No, no, I can't. They will kill me," he said.

"I'm the one that's gonna kill you right here," I said, pressing the gun in back of his knee.

He winced, anticipating the bullet. "Okay, okay. Don't shoot, I'll tell you. Kenny is hiding her at his apartment."

"That motherfucker!" I yelled, with a mixture of shock and rage. I staggered out of the van. "Gag them," I barked at Jimmy.

He grabbed duct tape off the rack and put it across their mouths. Both men were laying face down moaning on the van floor. I slammed the van's back door. "We have to get these guys to Morgan. I promised not to kill Viktor without permission."

"Permission? What do you mean?" He asked.

"That's what he said. I'm not fucking this up, just get in the van."

Jimmy climbed into the driver's seat and I got in on the passenger side. I held up the grenade and carefully put the pin back in. Jimmy's face went white as he held his breath, eyes wide with terror. When the pin was back in place he gasped and wiped sweat from his face.

"Get us back to the city fast," I said, as I took out my cell phone.

"You got it brother." He nosed the van into the street.

I called Morgan's number. After three rings he picked up.

"What's going on?" he said.

"Remember our last chat? I need your approval on one of my projects. Can you meet me now?" I asked.

"I'm at the hospital, but I'll meet you where we had our chat. I'm leaving now. Stay outside and wait for my call." Jimmy drove up 108th Street and took the ramp onto the Long Island Expressway. We headed west, opting to take the 59th Street Bridge to avoid tolls and cops.

Jimmy drove south on Second Avenue and made a right onto 35th Street. We parked on a side street near Ninth Avenue.

"Jimmy, you got cigs? I'm out," I asked, making a smoking gesture."

He took out his pack of Winston and handed me the pack and his lighter.

"Why would Kenny do that?" he asked.

"Kenny is out of his mind. He's been playing every angle and collecting money from the Mexicans and Russians. He sold me out to the Mexicans. Then, when they failed to kill me, he split the money with me. He probably has a deal with the Russians for part of Dana's ransom money," I explained.

"Before all this started, Kenny and I ripped off the Mexican heroin dealers that got you hooked. We stole their money and dope. Gave the money to Sullivan and sold the dope to the Russians for big money. Viktor didn't like the deal Dmitry made and wanted my share," I said.

"But maybe it was a set up by Kenny again," Jimmy said. "Kenny was the one that got me hooked on heroin. He gave me free samples and told me where to find more. I was fine with drinking and cocaine." He shook his head. "I had plenty of money to kill myself with that shit."

My phone went off. It was Morgan. "Can you come over and tell me what's going on?" he asked. "Don't bring any of your friends just yet," he added.

"Okay, I'll be there shortly," I said, and ended the call.

I turned to Jimmy. "Drive over to McKenzie's and park where I can see the entrance. I want to watch the front for a bit."

We headed over and parked up the block. We watched and waited for a while, but no one came in or out. The boys in the back started kicking against the van door.

"Cut it fucking out or I'll shoot both of you right here." I shouted.

They mumbled back at me, but the tape made it impossible to understand what they were saying. I looked over at Jimmy and noticed him tighten up on the steering wheel. His knuckles went white.

He tilted his head to the side, in the direction of McKenzie's. "Look."

I turned to look out the side window. Kenny walked up to the door and entered McKenzie's.

"This is fucking unbelievable. I'm going in," I said.

"Wait, what if this is some kind of set up?" he asked.

"If I'm not out in thirty minutes, come get me," I answered.

"They're not gonna let me take you out of there without a fight."

"Then you'd better get your head ready."

"This is gonna be bad," he said, firing up another cigarette and blowing the smoke out the window.

"It will only be bad if Morgan believes Kenny's bullshit. Keep these fuckers quiet until I come out."

I climbed out of the van, then hobbled across the street. As I approached the front door of McKenzie's, a cigarette glowed cherry red in the darkness. Whelan stepped out of the shadows and stamped out his cigarette.

"You ready for a little chat? Some things you've been involved in have gone south and it's time to do some explaining," he said, taking another step closer.

"That's what I've come to do. I have nothing to hide," I assured him.

Whelan opened the door and I walked into McKenzie's, not sure I would ever come out again. He followed me in and closed the door behind us.

The place was empty except for a couple of men drinking at one of the tables. Morgan and Kenny sat waiting in the back at Mr. Sullivan's table. I pulled out a chair and sat down. Whelan walked past the table and into the back room. "I'll be right back," he said.

I nodded a greeting to Morgan. His cologne was already suffocating me, even from across the table. He was dressed in a black blazer with a black button down shirt, his hands folded in front of him.

I turned to Kenny and he gave me a thin smile, then raised his eyebrows like this was a funny situation.

I turned back to Morgan. "So where do we begin?"

"Why don't you tell me what you know?" Morgan asked.

"I've been beaten within an inch of my life. I've had my girl kidnapped. My partner tried to kill me and steal my money." I explained.

Kenny looked like he was hanging on every word. As I described each event, his grin became larger, teeth showing in a full smile. He was completely amused by my accusations.

"I've followed all your instructions. Can I have your approval to take out Viktor?" I asked.

"I'll need more information than that, Bill," Morgan said.

Kenny interrupted. "I told Dmitry to abort the mission. He called Mikhail when we found out that Viktor gave us a bogus address. I have all your money right here. You're confused, Bill."

Whelan came out of the back and stood by Kenny. Arms crossed, his intimidating bulk casting a giant shadow on Kenny as he listened.

"I escaped with my life," I said.

"See, Bill? I told you that no one was going to kill you," Kenny said.

"Kenny handed me over to the Russians and took the ransom money that was meant to free Dana. She wasn't at the location where Kenny told me to pick her up. Viktor was ready to kill me and Mikhail put a shotgun to my back," I said.

Kenny's smile began to fade. The color left his face and for the first time ever he looked nervous. "They weren't supposed to hurt you," he said. Sweat began to bead up on his forehead and roll down the side of his face.

"Well, Kenny, I have a little surprise of my own. I've got a couple of your friends outside in the white van parked across the street."

Morgan looked up at Whelan. "Go check it out, Bran," he said.

Whelan walked over to the men sitting at the table and whispered something to them. Then he turned and walked out the front door. The men came over and stood by the table.

CHAPTER TWENTY-TWO

After a while Whelan came back to the table, but he appeared from the back of the restaurant, even though he had left through the front. He leaned over to Morgan and whispered into his ear.

Morgan stood up and walked into the back room. Whelan and the two other men stayed by the table. A few minutes later Jimmy and Morgan came out of the back.

"Jimmy told me what happened in Queens and the story checks out. I think we need a thorough discussion about tonight's events," Morgan said. "Jimmy, you're free to go," he added.

"I'm gonna have a couple of drinks at the bar," Jimmy said.

"That's fine. Kenny and Bill, you guys head into

the back so we can chat," Morgan said.

No one moved for what felt like five breaths. I could hear time pass as I watched eyes darting from face to face. Kenny made the first move and pulled out his gun. A sudden scuffle commenced with an explosive sound of breaking glass. Everything on the table went flying in the air. Chairs overturned and everything crashed to the floor.

The two men jumped him, but Kenny stepped back towards Whelan and was able to get a couple of shots off. Kenny turned and shot both men, and then Whelan moved with surprising speed for a man of his size and grabbed Kenny from behind. He put his massive arms around Kenny's neck and shoulders. Kenny struggled and kicked, but it was no use. Whelan squeezed tighter and tighter, until Kenny's head lulled to the side, his gun dropping to the floor. Whelan released Kenny and he collapsed to the floor like a ragdoll, his dead weight making a thudding sound.

Morgan looked at the injured men and signaled the bartender with a gesture to clean up the mess. On the floor one man was bleeding heavily from a stomach wound. The other guy was shot in the shoulder, but he must've hit his head on something as he fell to the floor. He was sprawled unconscious, lying next to the debris from the table.

Whelan dragged Kenny by the arm into the back. His shoes made a screeching sound as they scuffed along the polished wooden floor.

Morgan reached into his jacket and showed me a pistol butt in his waistband. "Come on Bill, let's sort this out." Then he reached over and took my gun from my waistband.

"Alright," I replied and followed along.

Out of the corner of my eye I noticed Jimmy watching from the bar. We traded glances and I noticed his hands were shaking. He took a hard drag of his cigarette and knocked back the rest of his drink. The last thing I saw as we left the main room was a grimace on Jimmy's face as he swallowed.

We walked downstairs to the lower level, through the stock room, and down another set of narrow stairs to the basement. Viktor was tied to a chair on a plastic tarp in the middle of the room. The only light in the room came from one conical lamp hanging over his head. A circle of light illuminated only his chair, the rest of the room remained in total darkness.

As I came off the last stair I noticed a line of chairs against the wall. Mikhail and Kenny were already sitting in the chairs, their hands and feet tied. Kenny was just starting to come around. Mikhail was staring at Whelan, terror in his eyes.

Whelan had his back to us, but spoke as if he was facing us. He took off his jacket, folded it carefully, and placed it on the table. Hanging from his belt was a holster, but it wasn't holding a gun; a huge knife hilt protruded from it. He rolled up his sleeves, adjusted his suspenders, and focused on preparing his tools at a table. "Come on in, Billy boy, and sit down. We've got work to do and no one is leaving until all questions are answered." His tone was almost joyful.

I sat in the chair at the end of the row, leaving an empty chair between Kenny and me. Morgan came over to tie me down; I didn't resist.

Viktor was unconscious, his chin resting on his chest. Whelan waved smelling salt under his nose. He coughed, gagged, and awoke gasping for air. He began to mumble in Russian, then bucked, trying to break free of the ties. He stopped abruptly when Whelan walked up to him and smacked him hard in the face.

"Speak fucking English, you Russian dog," Whelan snapped.

He returned to the table and took out a syringe and glass vial. Plunging the needle into the vial, Whelan carefully measured as he filled the syringe and pulled the needle out of the vial. He flicked the syringe and pushed the plunger. A small amount of liquid squirted out of the needle and into the air.

"You're going to feel a little sting. Then I'm going to ask you a few questions. If you're good, it will be quick, otherwise I can assure you that your death will be a slow and painful one," he said.

Viktor took a deep breath through clenched teeth as Whelan injected him with the serum. After a few minutes Viktor stopped struggling against his bonds.

"Where is Billy's girl?"

"She wasn't in the apartment when we grabbed Bill. I only wanted the money," he answered in a sleepy voice.

"What money?"

"One hundred thousand from the drugs we bought from Bill and Kenny."

"Why do you want that money?"

"Dmitry was an idiot. We paid way too much and I wanted half back. Kenny told me where to find Bill. We were going to rob and release him, but he wouldn't talk."

"Who shot Mr. Sullivan?"

"I didn't know he was shot. When did it happen?"

"Come on, son. You were doing so well. Don't ruin it," Whelan said. "Who shot Mr. Sullivan?"

"I don't know anything about that."

Whelan turned to the table, picked up a tool, and then stood in front of Viktor, blocking our view. Viktor started screaming and bucking against the chair. Bloody bits dropped to the floor at his feet. Whelan stepped back to the table and put down the tool. Several fingers on Viktor's left hand were bleeding. He whimpered and panted as Whelan busied himself at the table.

"Okay boyo, I'm gonna ask you again. Who shot Sullivan?"

"Ask Kenny. I don't know anything," Viktor replied.

"Why would Kenny know?" Whelan asked.

"Word on the street is that Kenny has many pans in the fire," said Viktor.

"Ah, so you do know something?" the big man said.

"No, no please. I don't know. I don't know anything," he pleaded.

Whelan stood in front of Viktor again, the screaming louder this time as he begged for him to stop. Bloody fingernails littered the floor, tapping as they hit the plastic tarp under the chair.

"Go easy on yourself, son. It's not worth it."

"No more, no more. I don't know," Viktor begged.

"Tell me what you know about Kenny's activities," Whelan said.

"He... He's in with us, and told the Mexicans..." Viktor said trailing off.

"Okay, so you're still holding out on me, aye?" he asked in a menacing tone.

Viktor shook his head frantically. He looked around for some kind of escape, but there was no hope. Whelan grabbed a pair of pliers off the table and straddled Viktor. An awful scream came out of Viktor that was not a human sound. Viktor tried to shake him off to no avail. Whelan pulled out four of Viktor's front teeth, one at a time. The bloody teeth dropped to the floor, bouncing as they hit the tarp.

Whelan got off of Viktor, and returned the pliers to the table. "I know you're ready now, son. Go ahead and tell me the rest."

He turned and patted Viktor on the back, and then walked over to Morgan.

"Get that idiot Jimmy to get rid of the van in the back. Someone might recognize it and we don't need any other visitors tonight."

Morgan straightened his suit blazer and left the room. He stared at Whelan's back for a few seconds a sour expression on his face. He wasn't used to taking orders from Whelan. Then he turned and stared at Kenny before leaving the room.

I heard a low sawing noise, but wasn't sure where it was coming from. Kenny was rocking slightly, his body pulsing in the chair. I realized as his hands came around and he continued cutting his bonds that Kenny was free.

Jumping up, he ran up behind Whelan and shoved

a knife into his back three times. Each thrust made a wet thud. Whelan grunted with each stab. He slid to the floor, and after a final gasp, he was still. Blood pooled beneath him and flowed under Viktor's chair.

At the sound of footsteps coming down the stairs, Kenny ran to the side of the stairs and pressed himself against the wall. He picked up his chair and swung it into Morgan's face as he walked into the room. Morgan crumbled to the floor in a heap.

Kenny slowly walked over to Morgan and kicked him in the face several times even though he was unconscious. Something ruptured with a sickening crack on the last kick.

Kenny bent over and took a gun out of Morgan's jacket. "I'll take this back now. It's my favorite gun," he said.

Then he walked over to Mikhail and cut him free. Mikhail rushed to the aid of his bloody friend in the center of the room, cursing in Russian as he untied his bonds.

Mikhail picked up Viktor. Bloody spittle oozed from his mouth, down his chin, and onto his shirt. I got one last look at Viktor's bloody face as Mikhail carried him towards the stairs. Kenny ran in front of them and glanced my way.

"Sorry, Bill, you're on your own." A grim smile crossed his face as they left the room.

Moments later three shots rang out, and then all was still. I bucked in my chair, trying to loosen the ropes that held me in place. I hoped I could break free by banging on the chair, but my struggles were fruitless. I continued to struggle, bucking and shaking the chair apart. The ropes started to cut into my wrists and I could feel blood dripping down into my hands. I pushed off the floor with all I had; the chair left the ground, tipping over. The last thing I saw was the floor rushing up to meet my face, and everything went black.

CHAPTER TWENTY-THREE

A small voice buzzed in my ear. It started as a whisper and became louder as I came back to consciousness. I blinked and slowly opened my eyes. My hands and feet were free. My head was wet and sticky with blood that was coming from a wound above my eyes. A face came into focus. It was Jimmy and he looked upset. "Are you okay? What the fuck happened?" He asked.

I was too groggy to reply, but sat up and looked around. Jimmy was over by Morgan, holding his head against his chest. Jimmy looked up. "He's still alive. We have to get him to the hospital."

"Are you kidding? He was going to kill me," I said.

"You don't know that for sure. I spoke to Morgan and he believed the whole thing. He just wanted to talk to you. Help me get him up," he said.

"They strapped me to a chair like the others. Whelan was going to torture all of us for info on Sullivan's assassins," I replied.

"Bill, come on. This is the only chance we have. Whelan is dead and if we can't save Morgan we're dead too. Sullivan will kill us if we can't do something to right this," he pleaded.

I tried to shake myself back from the pain in my head and I stood up. Spots of all different colors dotted in my vision. I became light-headed and dizzy, then quickly sat down before passing out.

"Dude, your face is all white. Stay here and I'll come back for you after I get Morgan to the hospital," he said.

"No, I'll try to help. And besides, I might need some attention too," I said.

I stood a little steadier on my feet and helped Jimmy carry Morgan up the stairs. Everyone upstairs was dead. Kenny had killed the bartender and the two injured guys. They laid sprawled, blood soaking their clothes and the floor.

We stepped over them and outside into the fresh

air. The lights glared and sparkled as my vision and mind cleared. Jimmy hailed a taxi and we jumped in. "Take us to the nearest hospital, quick. Our friend is hurt," he shouted.

The taxi driver started to give us some shit, so I gave him a wad of cash and he jammed on the gas, rushing us to the hospital.

Hours later, after they stitched up my forehead, I was sitting in the emergency room when Jimmy came and sat next to me. "The doctor says he might make it. His jaw and cheekbones are broken and his skull is fractured in a few places. They're not sure how much brain damage there is yet. He's going into surgery now to relieve the pressure on his brain," he said.

I heard every word, but the shock of the whole night was too much. The painkillers had made me dopey. "Thanks, Jimmy. You saved my life. I don't know how to thank you, but I'll find a way. Sorry, but I'm a little out of it from the meds." I said.

"We have to find Kenny and the Russians and find out who tried to kill Sullivan. If we can take care of this, Sullivan will have to take us seriously," he said.

"I heard Viktor confess to Whelan that Kenny

told the Mexicans where to hit Sullivan," I said.

"Holy shit, this is totally fucked up," he blurted.

"Kenny played every side, collecting money all the way. He used Rudy until he got caught, then blamed it on him. Whelan knew all about Kenny's ways, but I guess as long as he was a good earner, Sullivan kept him alive," I said. "Whelan was gonna kill us all, and once he had the information he wanted we were doomed. He knew Kenny set up Sullivan, but wanted to verify it."

"We need to check out Kenny's apartment. Dana might be there," Jimmy said.

"First we need to go to my place and get my Lincoln. I'm not taking taxis all over town," I said.

By the time we left the hospital, it was ten o'clock in the morning. The sun was shining, and it was a beautiful clear day. We grabbed a taxi and headed to my place. We picked up the car and drove up Broadway to Kenny's.

I double-parked and opened the door. "Keep an eye out for anyone we know. Call my cell if you see anything funny going on," I said.

"Here, take this," said Jimmy. He reached into his

jacket and handed me my gun. "I took it from Morgan. You might need it."

"Thanks Jimmy. If the cops tell you to move, just circle around the block."

As I headed for Kenny's building, I saw Dana coming up the block carrying a couple of grocery bags. She didn't look hurt or abused in any way. I took a step toward her, but then someone called out. She stopped, and a big smile lit up her face. My heart dropped as I saw Kenny come up and kiss her on the mouth. He took the groceries from her, and together they walked up the block looking very much like a couple.

I became overwhelmed by sadness. Feeling completely exposed, naked with confusion and embarrassed. I had to get out of there.

Jimmy got out of the car. "Why are you standing there? What's going on?" he yelled.

"Get in the car, we have to go," I said, wiping tears from my face.

Jimmy looked down the block and saw them coming. "What the fuck is this shit?"

"Just get in!" I shouted.

He got in and slammed the door. "Let's just shoot

the fucking bastard."

"I can't do this now. It's not the right time. Just drive."

Jimmy put the car in drive and stepped on the accelerator. "How can this be? I don't understand," I said.

I tried to shake myself out of the shock I was feeling. I felt like someone punched me hard in the gut. My whole world seemed turned upside down.

"They're a fucking couple. That motherfucker played me again, and he's been living with her the whole time I was out of commission. The Russians never had her."

"What about the proof of life picture on Dmitry's phone?" he asked.

"Kenny probably sent him a picture," I said, staring at the floor.

Jimmy looked around and then pounded the steering wheel. "This is a fucking mess," he said.

"Go east to NY Presbyterian. We gotta speak to Sullivan."

We were stuck in traffic near Fifth Avenue when I asked, "With Morgan down, who's taking care of things for Sullivan?"

"Mr. Sullivan's son Patrick came in from South Boston. He's been running that branch of the family business for years. Except Patrick has a reputation of flying off the handle and killing the messenger," Jimmy said.

"Great, this is just what I needed now. I thought Morgan was running things," I said.

"You'll see. Patrick's a real prick. He'll go ape shit when he hears about this bullshit with Kenny and the Russians. Man, he completely missed out on his old man's smoothness," he said.

We pulled up to the hospital at valet parking and climbed out. The attendant handed Jimmy a ticket and he gave it to me.

We walked into a huge lobby and towards an information desk. I asked what room Mr. Sullivan was in. The chubby blond receptionist said, "Visiting hours are over. Come back tomorrow at eleven o'clock."

Jimmy rushed over and pulled me back by the arm. "What are you doing? He's not in the regular wing. Follow me."

I followed Jimmy past the information desk and

down a long hallway to a bank of elevators. He pressed the button and we waited for it to arrive. After about fifteen minutes a bell sounded and the elevator doors opened.

We got out at the fourth floor, made a right, and walked past rooms packed with patients. Jimmy led the way past the nurses' station to a set of double doors at the end of the floor.

Inside the double doors was another short hallway. Three men stood up, looking very nervous.

Jimmy said, "We're here to see Mr. Sullivan, its important."

One guy stepped forward. "Wait here."

He knocked on the door and stepped in. A few minutes later someone else came out. This guy was short and stocky, and he looked like a younger version of Mr. Sullivan. Only this guy was chewing on a toothpick. He was dressed in a navy sports blazer with gold buttons, and a red Polo shirt underneath.

Jimmy stuck out his hand. "Hello, Patrick I'm Jimmy and this is--"

"Why the fuck are you idiots here?"

"We wanted to speak to your dad. We have a

problem," Jimmy tried to explain.

"Oh yeah, what's the problem?" he asked, taking the toothpick out of his mouth.

Jimmy explained what happened at McKenzie's. As Patrick Sullivan listened, his temper started to rise, and he reached into his jacket.

I jumped in. "Hold it Mr. Sullivan, we meant no disrespect. Jimmy saved Morgan, and me then brought us to the hospital. We needed your guidance."

"Who the fuck are you?" he asked, aggravated by my interruption.

"Sorry, sir. I'm Bill Conlin," I apologized.

"Oh, you're William Conlin? My dad's been telling me all about what a great job you've been doing. I heard about your trouble with the Russians," he said, his tone softening a little.

"This Russian thing has spilled over into McKenzie's. Kenny Shea killed Bran Whelan, put Morgan in a coma, and escaped with the Russians. Morgan told us to ask for permission before taking action. That's why we're here," I explained.

I thought he was going to shoot both of us when he reached into his jacket again. He took out his wallet, looked through it and gave me a card. "Call this number. Ask for Mrs. Goldberg and tell her you need some dry cleaning picked up. Give her McKenzie's address. Go there and wait. After everything is cleaned up, call my cell. The number is on the front of the card," he said.

"Thank you, sir. It was good to meet you," I said and shook his hand.

"Likewise," he replied.

I pulled Jimmy through the double doors and back to the elevators. We headed down into the lobby and smoked a cig while waiting for the valet to bring the car around. We didn't say a word to each other, trying to take in all that had happened.

CHAPTER TWENTY-FOUR

On the way back to McKenzie's I called the number Patrick Sullivan had given me. An older woman's voice answered.

"Goldberg's Cleaners, can I help you?"

"Hi is this Mi...Miss... Mrs. Goldberg?" I was stammering like an idiot, nervous about the whole mess.

"Yes, this is Mrs. Goldberg. How can I be of service?" she asked, with a polite disposition.

"We need some special dry cleaning picked up," I said, and gave her the address.

"I understand. How many suits do you need cleaned?"

I paused, mulling over the question. "Um, four suits," I answered.

"Is there a rear entrance?"

"Yes, there's a parking lot entrance on 39th near Ninth Avenue."

"Who will greet us?"

"I will. Bill," I replied.

"Very good. We will arrive in half an hour. Be outside waiting," she said. Then the phone went dead.

Morgan had about twenty keys on his ring, and it took a few minutes to find the right one for the back door. Inside, the bodies still lay where they fell. I could see the feet of one of the guys, surrounded by a large dark pool of blackish-red blood. A foul odor assaulted my senses and I began to dry heave.

"Oh god that's putrid!" I uttered, rushing to cover my nose and mouth.

"That's fucking horrid! Uh, like old pennies and shit!" Jimmy cried out.

I couldn't breathe and began backing up. "Let's wait outside," I said.

Jimmy ran out the back ahead of me, the door swinging closed behind him. I rushed outside after him, gagging and coughing. The air was sweet and fresh. We both took it in and tried to get ourselves under control.

We were sitting on the ground leaning against the wall when a white van pulled up. On the side of the van was a red decal that read "Mr. Speedy Cleaners," with a picture of a smiling guy, one thumb held up. Two fat guys in white overalls jumped out. "Which one of yous is Bill?" asked the driver. His voice was gruff, with a heavy New York accent.

"I am," I said, getting up off the pavement and brushing myself off.

"Okay here's da deal," he started to say.

"Where are Mrs. Goldberg's people?" I interrupted.

He scowled at me. "Don't ask any questions, she contracts these jobs out to us. Do we have your approval to begin?" he said, starting me down. Then he started over. "Okay here's da deal. No one comes in, and I mean *no one*. Anyone comes in while we're working and we'll be cleaning you up, too. Got it?"

"Got it," I said.

The cleaning guys opened up the back of the van and lowered an attached lift. They rolled out four large plastic containers, each about chest high and half-filled with some kind of liquid. It sloshed around as they moved them off the van and through the door.

I watched as they brought out a power washer gun attached to a motor on wheels, various cleaning supplies, two large pails on wheels with mops, a tray of spray bottles, and several large duffle bags. For fat guys they moved pretty quickly.

"Now lock her up after me and wait for me to bang on da door," the driver barked.

We sat outside waiting for what felt like hours. Cigarette butts peppered the pavement around us as we smoked and tossed the butts. The sun started to go down, and the light faded as the shadows disappeared.

"I'm out of smokes. You want anything?" Jimmy asked, as he started heading off to a deli up the block.

"Get me a pack of Reds and a regular coffee," I replied.

I watched Jimmy leave and wondered how much longer it would be before the cleaners finished.

A loud series of bangs startled me. "Come on, open up."

I unlocked the door and they came rushing out. In a mad scramble of activity they loaded everything back into the van. The last to come out were the plastic containers. Each time a container was brought out they struggled with its weight to get it onto the lift and into the van.

Jimmy came back just in time to see the last plastic container being loaded into the van. They closed the doors and jumped in without a word. The driver cooked the engine, it roared to life. As the van pulled away, we choked and coughed from the noxious exhaust fumes.

"Let's go in and see how they did," I said.

Jimmy stamped out his cigarette on the ground. "Let's check it out."

Inside, everything was completely cleaned up. The place was spotless. The only odor was a slight lingering aroma of pine. The place looked ready to open for business. I headed down the stairs to check on the sub basement, my legs aching.

I stopped in the storage room to give myself a break. A rush of memories flashed through my mind, images of the night I was tortured. I started to lose hope, as everything that kept me going seemed lost. The only thing I had left was a dull ache and a haunting feeling that I still had some tough decisions to make.

Taking a deep breath and letting it out slowly, I shook my head, trying to push the thoughts out of my mind. I had to refocus and take my life back. Anger welled up from the pit of my stomach. The anger turned into rage and I heard a distant sound, then realized it was my teeth grinding. The time had come to channel my rage into massive action.

Back upstairs; Jimmy was sitting at the bar, cigarette hanging from his mouth. A cloud of smoke floated in the air above his head.

I walked over to him, my boots thumping heavily on the wooden floor. "I see you're breaking the place in already?"

"Yeah, I think we deserve a few drinks. After all, we're still alive," he said, handing me a shot of Scotch.

He held up his glass. "Here's to killing those fuckers, every single one of them," Jimmy said.

We clinked glasses and knocked back our shots. The Scotch had a nice long oak finish, warming my chest and hanging on my breath for a few seconds. I picked up the bottle, poured another jigger into each glass, and we knocked back another round. I could feel the burn all the way down, and I relaxed a bit.

I called Patrick. "The dry cleaning has been picked up," I said.

"Good. Come by. We need to chat."

"Okay."

"And Bill, come alone this time," Patrick said, firm and short.

I paused trying to think why. "Okay, sir. On my way," I said and he ended the call.

"He wants to speak to me alone."

"I guess he doesn't like me much," Jimmy said.

"Let's lock up the place and I'll drop you at your apartment. Oh, one other thing. Find out if the Mexicans are still looking for me."

"It's been a pretty long time. They probably think you're dead or in hiding, but I'll ask around," Jimmy said.

"Don't let anyone know I'm back yet."

I took out the gun from my waistband, pressed the magazine release button, and it ejected into my hand. It was a double stack magazine and I checked the bullet count. It was full. Pointing the gun barrel towards the floor, I pushed the magazine back into the gun and heard it click home.

Jimmy watched me the whole time. When I finished we locked eyes and he nodded, cigarette ash dropping to the floor.

"C'mon, man, we just cleaned this place up and Patrick will be coming back soon."

"Wow, I didn't know you were such a clean freak."

"First impressions will go a long way with our new boss. Clean that shit up," I said, visibly annoyed.

Jimmy stepped on the ash and shuffled it around with his feet.

"How's that? Clean enough?" he asked, a thin, crooked smile crossing his face.

"That's just great. You're a real piece of work," I replied sarcastically.

"Thanks, brother. Let's go," he said, and walked towards the back door, leaving the bottle and glasses on the bar.

"Put this shit away," I barked.

"Okay, orders, orders," Jimmy said.

I sighed. Jimmy was starting to get back to his old self.

CHAPTER TWENTY-FIVE

I dropped Jimmy off, headed over to the hospital, and waited by Francis Sullivan's private room. Patrick came out, a toothpick in his mouth. He sat down next to me.

"There's a package waiting for you downtown. Go to the address on this card, and ask for Eddie Cohagen. Your instructions are in the package. Call me after you're done."

"Yes, sir," I replied.

I left the hospital and drove down to 20th and Eighth. The address on the card was the exact address of the police station where the FBI had held me. I parked a few blocks away and headed over.

Stepping through the main doors, I headed up two short sets of stairs and spoke to the officer at the front desk. He looked annoyed, but studied me for a few seconds. "What's going on?" he asked finally.

"I'd like to speak to Eddie Cohagen," I said.

"Who are you?" he asked.

"I'm Bill."

"You got a last name, Bill?"

"Conlin," I replied.

"Okay Mr. Conlin, have a seat. I'll check if he's available," he answered, narrowing his eyes.

He wrote in a journal on the desk and picked up a phone. "Yeah, there's a guy down at the front desk named Bill. Yeah, uh-huh right, got it." He hung up and looked at me like he was going to say something, but he didn't. He went back to writing in his journal.

The lobby of the precinct was closed off on both sides with metal doors. A square window with a metal mesh at eye level was the only way to see in or out. The doors had black scuffmarks all over the bottom half. I stared at the doors and noticed that they had been painted over many times; they were peeling, the old color showing through in spots.

My head was down and I was looking at my hands when a pair of black shoes appeared before me. I looked up to find a heavy-set man looking down at me. His head was buzzed close and his face unshaven. He wore a wrinkled gray suit.

"I'm Detective Cohagen. You wanna get some coffee?" he asked in a husky voice.

"Sure."

We strolled around the corner. I hoped for Starbucks, but Cohagen went into a small Indian deli and ordered two regular coffees.

He turned to me, and said, "So I hear you're a big war hero."

"Yeah, I saw some action," I said. "I don't know about the hero stuff."

"You're a very humble guy. I like that," he said, and handed me a coffee.

"Thank you."

"The sugar is over there," he said, and gestured to the right with his coffee cup.

I took a few steps, ripped open three packets of sugar, poured them in, stirred the coffee, and put the lid back on.

"Hey Julian, is it okay if I use the back room for a few minutes?" he asked the cashier.

"Sure, Eddie."

"C'mon, kid. Let's go have us a quick chat."

I followed Cohagen into the back of the deli to a refrigerated storage area behind the beverage cases. He sipped his coffee. "Sully asked me to dig up some info on that Mexican bitch, Angel. I'm trying not to get involved in this one cause the FBI is all over her ass. You can be sure that wherever she's going, they're watching. Someone left a package downtown and Sully wants you to pick it up."

He handed me a ticket.

"Bring this ticket to J.D.'s Pawn Shop on Canal Street. You'll pick up a black case with specific instructions inside. Don't come back to speak to me again and follow up with Sully after. The code to unlock the case is 711. Remember, you're gonna have to be real slick to pull this off with the way they're watching that bitch. She has some balls trying to kill Sully Senior."

He took another sip. "One other thing. Don't drag your ass on this cause there's this meeting tomorrow and Sully wants this all tied up fast."

"I understand, but what's your deal?" I asked.

"Sully and me go way back. We grew up together. I would do anything for him, but not this. It's way too hot. Be careful, kid. Anyone on the front of this one is likely to go down hard," he said, trailing off.

"I gave my name to the front desk officer when I came to speak to you. Is that gonna be a problem?" I asked.

"Nah, don't worry," Cohagen replied.

"Well, that desk cop wrote it down in a book. I saw him do it." "Not a problem, I'll take care of it. Those journals have a funny way of getting misplaced over time." He patted my back. "You pull this off and you're moving up, kid. Good luck."

We exited the deli. Cohagen went left and I went right. I got back in the Lincoln and drove down to Chinatown. I was hungry and couldn't pass up a chance to eat at an old favorite restaurant, 69 Bayard Street. The place had no curb appeal or atmosphere inside, just a bunch of small round tables, wooden chairs, and incredibly delicious food. I had pork fried rice and roast pork with tea.

When I finished, I headed out to the pawnshop. Peering in through the big glass windows, I expected to see gold on display, but all the shelves were empty. The main counter was unmanned so I tried to push open the door, but it was locked. Pulling back a step I noticed a doorbell and pressed it. I waited as dozens of people walked by me in both directions. An old Asian man appeared behind the counter and buzzed me in.

"What you want?" he asked as I stepped inside.

"I'm picking something up," I said, handing him the ticket.

He snatched the ticket from my hand and went into a back room. A few minutes later he emerged with a black leather brief case. He put on reading glasses to check that the ticket matched and cut off a tag. He slammed the case on the counter and shoved it in front of me. He stared into my face for a few beats. I reached into my pocket for some cash, but he waved me off.

"You leave now, we finished," he blurted, annoyed and agitated.

"Do I need to pay or sign anything?" I asked.

"No, too many questions. You just leave now."

The whole transaction was done in less than five minutes. The case was heavier than I expected.

Curiosity definitely had me, but with so many people around I'd have to wait to look inside.

CHAPTER TWENTY-SIX

I pulled into the garage of the uptown apartment and parked in the underground lot. It seemed odd that no one was in the garage, at the front door, or in the lobby. I got into the elevator and took it up to my floor.

When I got to my apartment, I found the door was open. I had an uneasy feeling that something was wrong. Putting the case down, I took out the Beretta from my waistband and switched off the safety. I moved the slide back and loaded a bullet into the chamber. The mechanism made a loud series of clicks in the dead silence. Fear gripped me, as beads of sweat formed on my forehead, and started dripping down my face.

I crept into the living room and glanced quickly

down the hallway, the Beretta held out in front of me as I searched each room. Moonlight came through the front windows and made it possible to barely make out the shapes of the furniture in the room.

The last room I checked was the small bathroom off the hallway. What I discovered was a gruesome scene. Jackie lay in the tub, her throat cut. Dark red blood had poured down her neck and chest. Her crystal blue eyes stared lifeless at the ceiling.

All of a sudden I felt sick, my legs shaking beneath me. Leaning over the sink, I vomited. I wiped my mouth, lifted my head to look in the mirror, and noticed my face was white as a ghost. I splashed my face and neck with cold water.

Out of the corner of my eye I spotted Mikhail rushing at me, a thin wire wrapped around his hands. I stuck up my left hand just in time to block him from strangling me. It didn't stop him from pinning my hand to my face, and I dropped the gun to the floor as I started to lose my balance. Using all my force, I swung a series of elbows into his mid section. Mikhail gritted his teeth, squeezing harder, and continued to hold on as I bucked. The wire started to cut into the side of my neck, and I could feel blood dripping onto my collarbone.

I spun around to face him and knee him in the balls. Mikhail let out a big sour breath of air with a grunt, and then dropped to the floor coughing, taking me with him. Still unwilling to let go, Mikhail continued pulling the wire tighter, cutting deeper into my neck and pinned hand.

The room started to grow dark. Multi-colored spots appeared in my vision. Time was running out. Struggling to get my right hand into my pocket, I pulled out my keys and plunged one into his eye. Mikhail screamed and released the wire as he grabbed for his impaled eye. He yanked out the keys and rolled on the floor howling in pain.

Crawling back into the bathroom I went for the gun. I picked it up, turned and fired at Mikhail. He scrambled on the floor, heading for the door. Bullets bounced off the doorframe and exploded with splinters as my shots went wide. I staggered out of the bathroom and squeezed off three quick shots. Mikhail crumpled to the floor, groaning and gasping for air, blood pouring out of his wounds.

After a few breaths he rolled over onto his back, let out a final breath, and was still. His right eye oozed blood and eye jelly down the side of his face. I slid against the wall and down to the floor, panting and soaked with sweat. Putting my hand to my throat, I felt the cuts around my neck. My hands came away wet with blood. No cut veins or arteries, but dangerously close.

I called Patrick Sullivan. "I'm sorry to bother you, sir, but I have a situation at my apartment. The neighbors have probably already called the police."

"Say no more and stay put," he said, and ended the call.

Thirty minutes later a knock came at the door. "Police, open up. We've received a call," the officer said through the door.

"I'm coming," I shouted, and took a deep breath wondering if I was going to jail.

I looked through the peephole and saw a police badge. Sighing I unlocked the door and opened it. To my surprise Detective Eddie Cohagen walked into the room alone. He closed and locked the door behind him. Disgust and displeasure was written all over his face.

"It seems that I'm gonna have to work with you against my better judgment," he said, taking off his sunglasses.

He stepped over Mikhail's corpse. "How can I be of service, kid?" he asked.

"Check out the bathroom," I said.

He strolled down the hallway avoiding the dark, pooling blood.

"Now that's a damn shame, wasting a pretty lady like that. Some people have no appreciation for beauty," he said.

"It's a total waste of life and for what? All this was just to get back at me," I said, trying to hide my sadness and exhaustion.

"I guess you know the reason for this aggression," Cohagen said.

"Kenny Shea sold me out to gangs that wanted me dead. He's in with the Russians and the Mexicans," I said, through clenched teeth.

"Yeah, I've been hearing that name a lot lately. It seems he's pissed off a bunch of people, but it won't matter."

"Why?"

"That, my friend, is because, he is way up the FBI's ass. The brass downtown ordered hands off on Kenny Shea. He's an informant on some big sex-trafficking ring up from Mexico," he replied now nervous, his eyes darting around the room.

"So you mean to tell me we can't do a thing? Even though he tipped off the Mexicans so they could get to Sullivan?" "Look, kid, you and I are soldiers and we do whatever we're told. It's that simple, just follow orders and stay alive."

"That is fucking balls," I barked, frustrated.

"Of course there is one problem," he said, scratching his beard.

"What's that?"

"Sully will pull your plug if you don't follow orders and the police brass won't," he said.

"Now I feel a whole lot better," I said, sarcastically.

"Okay kid, here's the deal. I'll take reports from the neighbors and squash this as a robbery attempt. You call the cleaners and get back on track for our meeting tomorrow."

"Our meeting? I thought this was too hot for you?"

"It appears that Sully wants me in, and he doesn't give a shit how I feel about it. I'll give you a call in the morning. Here's my card, the number is on the back. I already have your cell number."

Cohagen put his sunglasses on, smiled, and stepped over Mikhail again on his way out. As he left he looked back and shook his head before closing the door. "Damn shame, fucking foreigners are ruining our country." I went into the kitchen, took out a glass and the bottle of Knob Creek, then poured three fingers worth. I swallowed too big of a gulp and coughed as the bourbon burned all the way down.

I thought about Jackie. What a waste. It saddened me that I caused so many deaths. Anger and rage welled up from a dark place in the pit of my stomach and I squeezed my fists tight trying to ease the tension. My knuckles cracked, the sound bringing me back. I released my grip and the tension eased as the bourbon finally kicked in.

Could I let Kenny and Dana go on and live happily ever after?

Not a chance.

Did Viktor suffer enough for what he did to me? Not even close.

Viktor and Kenny destroyed my life, and now it was my turn to destroy them.

I called Mrs. Goldberg and asked to have two suits picked up. I took out my lighter, lit up a cig, and blew the smoke out through my nostrils slowly. After a few more sips of bourbon I tried to relax, but I became agitated and decided to let out my rage on Mikhail's lifeless body. I kicked his corpse in the ribs, making a sickening thud each time. After three kicks my anger subsided.

A loud bang at the door snapped me out of my drunken thoughts. "Yeah, who is it!" I yelled, not bothering to get up off the floor.

"It's the cleaners."

I stumbled over to the door. Looking through the peephole I recognized one of the guys that had cleaned McKenzie's. Opening the door I walked back into the kitchen and picked up the bottle off the floor.

The larger guy came in first, barreling into the apartment with a very large case on wheels.

"You could definitely fit two bodies in that," I said, under my breath.

"Excuse me?" he said as he turned around to help his partner in with the rest of the supplies.

"Forget it," I said, taking a swig from the bottle and wiping my mouth with the back of my hand.

"Wait out in da hallway. We'll let you know when you can come back in," he said.

I left the apartment and the door was quickly shut and locked behind me. Leaning against the wall I slid down to the floor and took another big swallow from the bottle. The hallway was quiet and empty.

An electrical buzzing sound like a coffee grinder came from behind the door. The thought of what they were doing made me want to throw up. Covering my ears with both hands, I hoped to block the sound, but it crept past. It started to drive me crazy, so I got up and paced the hallway. After two hours the door opened and the cleaners left, pushing the giant case down the hallway and into the elevators.

When I entered the apartment, the aroma of pine was heavy just like at McKenzie's. The bodies, blood, and gore were all gone. They even cleaned my ashtray, which sat shiny and empty on the counter. The black leather case waited where I left it, untouched. Picking up the case, I walked into the kitchen and dropped the empty bourbon bottle into the sink. I collapsed onto the couch, put the case on the coffee table, turned on the TV, and passed out cold.

CHAPTER TWENTY-SEVEN

Sunlight coming through the windows woke me up. I opened my eyes and tried to remember where I was. The memories of Jackie in the tub, her throat cut, and fighting Mikhail to keep him from strangling me rushed through my mind.

I felt my neck and the dried blood from where Mikhail had tried to strangle me. I squeezed my eyes tight, pushing the grisly visions from my mind, but it didn't work. They floated behind my eyes with each blink or glance.

The TV was still on so I watched, hoping for a distraction. A news anchor yammered on about President Obama's trip to Israel. The case still sat on the coffee table, calling me to open it. Getting up off the couch I walked into the kitchen to make some coffee. I dreaded opening the case, but time was almost up. I couldn't image what kind of fucked up job I had to do next.

After my second cup, I decided it was time to face the music. I opened the case and immediately knew what it was. The only thing missing was the plastic explosives. Apparently Patrick had known I had some in the armoire. Next to the mechanism was a wireless detonator with a trigger switch. It could be detonated from a distance, but probably not from far enough to make a clean get away. I was up to my knees in shit with the Mexicans again.

The instructions stated that a meeting was taking place at one o'clock this afternoon in the same Argentinean restaurant where I saw Kenny and Angel. There were pictures of Angel and her black Range Rover, showing the license plate. Patrick wanted Angel blown to pieces, and wanted me to place the bomb under her SUV.

I couldn't believe I had a crooked cop for a partner. Cohagen said there would be a big promotion in it for me. Was he full of shit? I really didn't have a choice. It was kill or be killed.

The phone went off, vibrating on the coffee table. It was Cohagen. "You ready kid? I'll pick you up in front of your building in fifteen minutes. Make sure everything is set up properly, we don't need any accidents. I heard you have a knack for this stuff."

"See you in a few." It was time to arm myself to the teeth. I went to the armoire in the bedroom and unlocked it. The Beretta was too big, so I opted for a Glock. It had a smaller profile and was just as effective. I loaded two extra clips and placed them on the bed.

Pulling open the drawer, I selected a small combat knife and strapped it to my wrist. The last drawer contained explosives. I slid it open and looked at C4 on the left and grenades on the right. I removed a square of C4 and two grenades and placed them on the bed. I locked up the armoire, walked back into the living room, picked up the case, and brought it into the bedroom. Once I finished setting up the C4, I took out the detonator and locked the case.

I didn't have much time left, but I needed a shower to regroup. After five minutes of scalding hot water, I was ready.

I dried off, and put on black jeans, a white shirt,

and black boots. Just as I was trying to decide whether to shave off my beard, the phone started buzzing. Ignoring it, I brushed my teeth, put gel in my hair, and combed it back. Looking up from the sink, I had one last glance in the mirror, dark circles under blood shot eyes, and a straggly beard. I scanned down to the cuts on my neck and pulled up my collar. My face looked like shit, but my gelled dark hair gave me a little style.

I took in a deep breath and let it out slowly. "You can do this."

The phone started buzzing again. I picked it up this time. "Yeah."

"How long you gonna keep me waiting down here?" Cohagen asked.

"I'm coming down now, just had to finish up." I said and gathered my things.

I exited the building with the black leather case in my hand. The October air was cool, the fall season in full swing. A breeze blew out of the west and I closed my eyes, feeling the wind on my face, listening to the rustling leaves. I gazed up. There wasn't a cloud in the sky. It was a beautiful day.

A black Ford sedan with dark tinted windows sat

at the curb. The passenger window rolled down "C'mon kid, let's go," Cohagen called out. I got in the car. "I picked up some coffee at the deli. You like regular, right?"

"Yeah that's fine," I said.

"We need time to get a good spot and check things out. I wanna be able to see the block before our special guests arrive."

Cohagen pulled away from the curb and nosed the black sedan into traffic. He had the radio tuned to 1010 WINS news. The top story, several bodies found in a Brooklyn parking lot. When we arrived at our destination, Cohagen circled around for a while until he found a parking spot with a full view of the restaurant. We watched and waited.

At 12:50, Angel sat in the front seat of her Range Rover, watching people pass on the street. The busy city folk rushed around, shopping or grabbing food on their lunch breaks.

A few minutes later she got out of her car and stood in front of the steak house. The restaurant door opened, and a familiar face appeared. Fat Paco. He whispered in her ear. She nodded and entered the restaurant. He stayed outside, watching the street and her SUV.

"Well kid, it looks like things just got a whole lot harder for you. They're watching Angel's ride," Cohagen said, taking a sip of his coffee.

I opened the case and took out the detonator. "Let's rock!" I said, putting the detonator in my pocket and jumping out of the car.

Crossing the street was the easy part. A city bus roared by and I used the distraction to quickly get close enough to Angel's car. I walked low and pushed the case under the back bumper, then scurried off in reverse, never looking back to see if anyone noticed me.

It was 1:15 when I got back in the sedan with Cohagen.

"That was pretty smooth, considering that fat guy is scanning the street," he said.

Time slowed down to a crawl. I could feel each minute tick by, my ears burning with a stress fever that left my face dripping with sweat. The clock on the dash showed 1:25; I took out the detonator and held it. At one 1:28 I looked at the dash and wiped the sweat from my face with the back of my sleeve. When 1:30 came my hands also started sweating and the detonator became slippery.

A white van pulled up and double-parked a few cars in front of Angel's SUV. "What the fuck is this?" I said, knowing that this was either more Mexican gangsters or FBI agents.

"I don't know kid, but we are running out of time. This place is getting too hot," Cohagen replied.

"She's gotta be coming out soon. This must be some kind of escort," I said aloud to myself.

Paco held a phone to his ear and dark suits came out of the white van. They stood beside him as Angel came out of the restaurant.

"This is it! C'mon kid, press the button," Cohagen shouted.

Once Angel was in the Rover, Paco got in the white van with the suits and eased forward a little.

"Hurry, press it!" He urged.

I had my thumb ready to press the button when I saw something that stopped me cold. A sudden chill went down my spine as Angel's little girl popped her head up in the back window. She had a doll in each hand and was playing. I could see her cute little face smiling as she pretended the dolls could speak.

Fear and horror rattled through my mind. I shook my head in disbelief, and started yelling, "No this can't be happening!" But it was happening and I couldn't look away.

I panicked as the Rover started to pull out of the spot, and Cohagen shouted, "Press the fucking button! Press it!"

"No! We can't! There's a little girl. We have to abort!" I pleaded.

Cohagen reached over and squeezed my hand setting off the case. I screamed, "No!"

It was too late. A tremendous explosion rocked the street, with a deafening crash. Cars and store windows shattered on both sides of the block. The impact shook the sedan, and pieces of the Rover tumbled down from the sky and dropped all over the street. It was like air support in Afghanistan, FA-18 fighter jets that bombed targets while we fought it out in a small city northeast of the war zone. Our missiles hit too close to our position and friendly fire killed many of my battle buddies. I felt drained and helpless as I watched the smoking wreck.

I snapped out of it when Cohagen pulled out his service revolver and pointed it at my face. I was looking down the barrel of a steel blue snub-nosed .38 police special.

"Now I'll get the promotion and you're fucked. You're under arrest for the murder of Armando and Angel Sanchez. You have the right to remain silent…"

Deciding I wasn't going to be arrested, I grabbed his wrist, pointing the gun away from me and smashing his hand hard against the dash several times. Cohagen grunted as the gun dropped to the floor.

Pulling my hand into my sleeve, I managed to get the combat knife out and sliced Cohagen's wrist deep before grabbing his head. I rammed his face into the steering wheel with all my force, again and again, until he stopped moving.

Cohagen leaned over the steering wheel a bloody mess, his sunglasses bent, with shards of glass sticking out of his face. I bolted out of the passenger side and came around to the driver's door. I dragged Cohagen's unconscious body out of the sedan and got in the driver's seat. I cooked the engine, threw the car in gear, stamped on the accelerator, and peeled out, tires smoking. People were running and screaming all over the block.

The white van didn't explode, but was thrown onto its side, hitting some parked cars from the impact. As I sped off I could see the suits scrambling around the burning hulk of Angel's Range Rover. They tried to help, but the smoke and heat from the fire kept them back.

I didn't have much time, but needed to get my money and supplies before the FBI tried to arrest me again.

CHAPTER TWENTY-EIGHT

Before I ditched the sedan I called Jimmy, and rambled on about the job gone wrong. "The job was fucked, I should've known it. Cohagen killed the little girl, he fucking killed her. Oh my God, that poor little girl. What the fuck was she doing there?"

"Bill, what are you talking about? What job? What girl? Have you lost your mind?"

"That fucking crooked cop tried to set me up, but I got him good." "Okay, calm down and tell me slowly so I can understand" he said.

I told him everything and he was quiet for a minute. "Why would she bring her kid along?" he asked.

"I don't know, but it's fucking crazy," I blurted.

"How do you know Patrick was in on the frame

up? You gotta call him," Jimmy reasoned.

"I can't. I gotta get out of town now. I need your help. I need someplace to go and a way out fast."

"Okay, stay calm. I'll meet you at a bar on Ninth and 44th. Odin's Hall," Jimmy said, in a calm tone.

I left the sedan by a park on 18th Street and rushed uptown to my apartment. There I found two black duffle bags in the closet. Unzipping the bags on the bed, I opened the armoire and loaded in weapons and supplies. In the one bag I put several handguns, a couple boxes of bullets, grenades, knives, and explosives. If a war was coming I had to have a mobile arsenal.

In the other bag I dropped in the rest of my money, around fifty thousand dollars, and some clothes. I headed into the bathroom and shaved my face and head. I raced out to meet Jimmy. Odin's Hall had that trendy bar feel with a polished wooden bar, a giant mirror sitting behind racks of high-end booze, and framed pictures of old Manhattan on the walls. Full-length windows gave a panoramic view of the street from anywhere within. I entered and sat on a stool at a small wooden table against the wall. I faced the street and eyed the front entrance. As I scanned the interior I noticed that they had a good selection of bourbon.

A very attractive young waitress came over and looked down at my bags before taking my order. She wore blue jeans and a short sleeve white top that clung and emphasized her small perky breasts. Her dark blond hair was pulled neatly into a bun. She had a pretty long neck and hanging earrings.

I guess I stared a little too long while I pondered her beauty and she let out a slight giggle. "Good afternoon. Are you staying for lunch?" she asked.

"No, just some Knob Creek, please. About three fingers. And some ice water." I replied.

"Okay, I'll be right back."

She came back after a few minutes with the drinks on a tray and placed them on the table.

"Are you sure you don't want to hear our specials? Some food might help a little."

I felt completely depressed and worn out as I took a sip of the bourbon. I probably looked like a wreck. "Maybe when my friend gets here. I'm okay for now."

Her eyes darted to my black duffle bags. "Are you

traveling today? Oh sorry, didn't mean to pry," she said, smiling.

"Yeah, I've had enough of this town for a while."

"This city can wear on your nerves. Sometimes I feel like running away to a new city or country," she said.

I wanted to be polite and buy some time without being rude, so I asked for the menu.

"Here you go," she said, perking up. She placed the menu on the table.

"I'll give you a few minutes."

I took another sip and pretended to look for something to eat while I reflected on the recent events. Sadness overwhelmed me as visions of the little girl flashed in my mind. Her apple cheeks, bright eyes, and vibrant smile. So innocent, so fragile. Tears welled up in my eyes; pain and anguish filled my thoughts. Another wasted life and for what? All to help kill low-life bottom feeders. I should have killed that fucking cop.

I hit the bourbon again and swallowed a big gulp. The burn immediately snapped me out of the grief as I choked and coughed. Jimmy came rushing into the bar and walked right past me into the back. He turned around and sat at the bar.

"Don't you even recognize your own cousin?" I barked.

"Holy shit, Bill. I thought you were some Neo Nazi or something. Where did all your hair go?"

"I guess the new look is working then," I said

"Let's get out of here. You can't be on the street. I know a place you can stay for a while," Jimmy said.

Jimmy picked up one of my bags. Finishing what was left of the bourbon I put a twenty under the glass and walked out.

Jimmy hailed a taxi and we headed up to the West 80s. He paid the driver and I followed him down a ramp to a basement apartment. The smell of urine assaulted my senses. Any slightly hidden space in the city was fair game as a bathroom for street people. Jimmy ignored the odor, took out keys, and opened a heavy metal barred storm door. Behind it was another door, also made of metal. He unlocked three dead bolts and we entered.

"This is Tracy's old apartment. We never got rid of it. You never know when you might need a place to crash," he said.

It was far from what I had expected. I thought it would be a dump like Jimmy's old apartment, but once inside it clearly had a women's touch. In the main room sat a nice couch with a floral pattern and a patterned rug. On either end of the couch were small end tables with nick-knacks and coasters. On the walls were framed pictures of flowers and birds. It had a small clean kitchen and bedroom, complete with floral comforter and matching skirt.

"Wow, Tracy really knows how to dress up an apartment. I thought this was a total dump from the outside," I said.

"Yeah, Tracy's a real keeper. She really helped me to clean up and learn to be proud of myself," Jimmy said, with a slight smile.

"I have to speak to Dana before I leave."

"I don't think that's a good idea, Bill. She's living with Kenny, and I'm not sure that talking to her is going to win you any points after all this time," he said.

Jimmy pulled out his lighter and lit a cig. "Here's what I found out about Viktor. He left the country and is now in Russia living with his brother. Viktor's brother is a big wig in the Russian mob, based somewhere outside Kiev. Dmitry's gone back to being in charge of the Brooklyn area. The civil war between the groups was crushed once Viktor left to hide under his brother's wing."

"I don't care where he is or who's wing he is hiding under, I'm gonna kill the fucker for ruining my life," I said, through gritted teeth.

"Hold out here for a few days, until we can get a plan together," Jimmy said.

"I can't fly out of any major airports or go through customs. The FBI will be looking for me. I need a way out where no one will notice," I said.

"I know this guy who works on the docks. Give me a day or two to check on a couple of things and for fuck's sake stay out of site," he said.

"Okay, I'll try."

"You better, because if they find you it will lead to me and Tracy. Then we're all fucked. I'll be back tonight with some food. Just try to forget about today the best you can," Jimmy said.

He walked out and I locked the door behind him.

CHAPTER TWENTY-NINE

I sank into the couch and buried my face in my hands. I was filled with sadness. Thoughts of self-pity swirled through my mind. Lifting my head, I leaned back and stared at my hands. I searched the lines of my palms for some kind of sign that my life would change for the better. I turned them over and followed the veins to my fingernails dirty with dried blood around the edges. I felt another wave of sadness wash over me; large tears fell from my eyes. I was reminded of the senseless death of an innocent little girl.

The sound of my phone vibrating on my hip snapped me out of the gloom. It was Patrick Sullivan. I blinked at the phone trying to decide whether to answer. "Yes?" I said.

"Bill, what's the deal?" Patrick asked.

"The job is complete," I said, not offering any details.

"Yeah, but Eddie was found dead on the street. He bled out from glass cuts. His car was located abandoned on the West Side, only a few minutes ago."

"We were too close to the blast and glass from the impact cut him up. The place was crawling with FBI agents and I had to get out of the area quickly," I said.

I should have known that Eddie would screw this up. He always had a way of complicating things. Even when we were kids he pulled this kind of shit. Meet me and I'll compensate you for your troubles," he said, sincerity in his voice.

"I have some loose ends to take care of first," I said.

"I understand. Well, whenever you're ready you'll have a job in our organization. I'll hold your payment. You've proven that you can be counted on in the last few days. Be on alert, our contacts say a Latino FBI agent has a real hard on for you."

"I will, sir," I said, and ended the call.

I went into the bathroom and striped off my clothes. Inside the bathroom a colorful striped patterned shower curtain and plastic liner closed off a clean tub. I peeked in, berry shampoo and lime-scented body wash sat against the white tiled back corner. After turning on the hot and cold water, the pipes made a high pitched whining sound. The room filled quickly with hot steam. I pulled the curtain back and stepped in, then sat on the tub floor. Letting the hot water hit the back of my head was the relief I sought. The fruity shampoo and body wash added a refreshing surprise to the shower. When I was finished, I used clean towels that were stacked neatly under the sink.

The night was uneventful and I searched the apartment for some beer or alcohol, but found none. Instead I settling down on the couch to watch some TV and quickly fell asleep.

In the morning Jimmy called and startled me awake. "Hey, what's up?"

"I'll be by with some coffee and egg sandwiches in a little bit. How did you hold up last night?" he asked.

"Just fine. Please tell Tracy how much I appreciate the use of her apartment."

"I will. And I'll see you shortly."

Jimmy arrived a few minutes later and we sat in

silence, eating the sandwiches and drinking coffee. It wasn't the best breakfast, but the kindness went a long way.

"I've put in a call to this guy I know," Jimmy said. "Blake Miller. He works on the docks in Brooklyn and Newark. He knows someone that can help and he'll tell us next steps tomorrow."

"I still have some loose ends to take care of first," I said.

"What the fuck Bill? You can't just walk around. The cops will pick you up."

"Even you couldn't recognize me yesterday. And you're my cousin," I said.

"That's true, but it just makes me nervous. I'm sticking my neck out pretty far, but do what you have to," Jimmy said.

"Believe me, getting shot or going to jail is not on my list."

"I'll come back tonight with more food, cigarettes, and bourbon. Whatever you do, don't get followed back here. I'll see ya later and good luck," Jimmy said. He walked out, slamming the door behind him.

I finished the coffee and got dressed. Needing

some exercise, I strolled down to Bryant Park hoping to see Dana. There were cops everywhere, but none recognized me with my new look. The business crowd and tourists rushed around on the street so I was able to use them for cover.

When I arrived at Bryant Park I sat on a bench and watched people having lunch. Sitting there brought back memories from a different life, when things were simpler. Before I started working for Sullivan and lost Dana.

I decided that I needed proof that Dana and I were finished. I headed into the restaurant and asked the host about Dana.

"She's working the second shift tonight" he said.

I could tell that he really wasn't sure giving out her information was a good idea. "Please tell her Bill came by," I said, and I left.

The sun was now dead center in the sky. Small white puffy clouds slowly changed shape as they moved south.

Since I had the information that Dana was still in town and working, it was time to stakeout her apartment. If I could catch a glimpse of Kenny I might be able to close up a big loose end.

An hour later I was on Dana's block, looking in the window of a mobile phone store when I saw Kenny come out of her building. He looked around, his senses on high alert. I followed him from the opposite side of the street as he walked towards the park. He turned the corner onto Central Park West and walked toward his grey Mercury parked on the street. I came up fast, as he took out his keys to unlock the driver side door. He accidentally dropped his keys; bending down to pick them up off the pavement and that was all the time I needed.

I shoved my gun hard into his back, "Hey, remember me?" I said.

He let out a grunt. "Yeah, I thought you might come looking for me, but I did leave you alive at McKenzie's. Remember?"

Reaching into his jacket, I grabbed his gun. "You won't need that. We have a few old debts to settle. Now get into the car, or I'll shoot you here," I growled.

Kenny lowered himself into the front seat. I opened the back door and climbed in behind him. I pressed the gun to the back of his neck. "Start the engine. We're going for a little ride," I said.

He did as he was told and I leaned back in the seat, the gun pointed at the back of his seat.

"Is this about money?" he asked.

"No, this is about how you ruined my life and stole my girl."

"You can't kill me. I'm an undercover FBI agent. If I'm found dead there's nowhere in the world for you to hide," he said, brimming with confidence.

"There won't be a body. Now, let's go," I said, with a sneer.

He put the car in gear and turned the steering wheel. Suddenly he bolted out of the car. As he rushed out I squeezed off two quick shots clipping him in the shoulder. Blood sprayed onto the dash and window, but it didn't stop or slow him down. The car rolled a couple of feet and bumped into the parked car in front, then stopped.

He ran across the street towards Central Park and was hit by a passing car in the opposite lane. He bounced onto the hood, his body shattering the windshield. He rolled off the other side and kept running.

I jumped out of the car, and went after him, but couldn't get a clear shot with all the people standing around the crashed car. Kenny ran to the waist-high grey brick wall that surrounded this section of Central Park, and hurdled over the wall down into the woods. When I reached the wall and looked down Kenny was rolling and skidding down the tree-studded hill, deep into the park. I stopped to gather myself and looked down, a trail of blood led to where Kenny had hopped over the wall. I had to go after him, but not now. With my legs aching, I could never catch him.

I got into Kenny's car and drove off around the block. Parking Kenny's car a few blocks away, I walked back to Dana's to tell her the truth about Kenny, and his web of lies that had ruined my life.

I arrived at the front door to Dana's building and pressed the button to her apartment. When no one responded I stood there and wondered what my options were and then tried again. There still was no response. Finally a young couple came out and I was able to hold the door. I don't know why, but they let me in without question. Didn't anyone in this building care about safety?

I went up the stairs to Dana's apartment and knocked on the door. Dana opened the door her hair wrapped in a towel.

"What did you forget your keys again? Oh sorry, can I help you?" Dana said a little embarrassed.

"It's Bill. I know I look different, but can we talk for a few minutes?

"Bill? Oh my God! What do you want?" she asked.

"I wanted to tell you the truth. Can I please come in?" I asked.

"Okay, just make it fast. I'm expecting someone," she said.

I sat on her couch and she went into the bedroom.

"Give me a couple of minutes to get dressed and I'll be right out," she shouted from the other room.

After a few minutes she came out and sat next to me on the couch. "So what's up? I don't have much time, before I have to get ready for work," she said.

I looked into her beautiful green eyes. "I worked with a guy when we first met, and he sold me out to some bad people. They kidnapped me, and beat me so bad I was in a coma for months. After rehab I was able to get back on my feet. I thought of you the whole time, I thought they had grabbed you too. That guy is Kenny, and you're living with him now. He's a crooked FBI agent and I'm here to tell you that…"

She cut me off, her face changing to a sour, angry expression.

"Listen Bill, you made up these crazy stories about people chasing you, and then you disappeared. Even when we were together you were unreliable and now you're stalking me. I don't even know a Kenny."

"The guy you're with is my old partner Kenny. I don't know what name he's using now. He's ruined my life by double-crossing me several times. He's dangerous, a dirty informant for the FBI and a con man. He plays games with everyone he comes in contact with. You have to believe me."

"I'm not listening to this nonsense anymore. You need to leave now."

"Dana, I'm not making this up. You have to get away from him. The Irish Mob is looking for him. He helped a rival gang try to kill their Boss, Please listen."

She stared at me, her face filled with pity and disgust. "I don't believe you. I don't want to hear anymore. Now get out." "But, Dana please, everything

I've done over the last year has been to come back to you. You have to listen. You're in danger." She stood up, with a frightened look and screamed, "Get out! Get out or I'll call the police!"

"Okay I'll leave, but check things out for yourself and you'll find things don't add up." I turned to look at her one last time before leaving. "I'm sorry Dana. I wish this made sense. It is a crazy story and it's what my life has become. I hope you can find your own truth," I said, and turned away.

I headed down the stairs, a heavy cloud of sorrow hanging over my head. I couldn't expect a normal person to believe events that only happened in the movies. Dana closed the door behind me and she didn't say another word. The door closed with a quiet click and the sound of deadbolts being turned only added to the closure. I continued out into the cruel city that brought me to this devastating moment.

CHAPTER THIRTY

I walked back downtown towards my hiding place. After a few blocks the sky became gray and overcast. A low rumble of thunder was followed by cold rain that soaked me to the bone.

The gloom of the day's events was only compounded by the dreary weather. I cursed at the sky, letting out a primal scream filled with anger and pain. The rain continued splashing my face as large drops mingled with tears. I swore to myself that Kenny and Viktor would pay for what they had done.

When I got back to Tracy's apartment, I was completely soaked. I dried off, changed, and sank into the couch. Time slowed to a crawl and I stared at a muted TV, mind blank, listening to the rhythm of my breathing. A bottomless depression left me rattled and turned my stomach. I wanted to puke, but I was empty.

When I was recovering from my injuries I thought that everything would be all right. I dreamed of a day when I could rescue Dana and start over.

Dana never knew what had happened to me. Was it really so unbelievable that a dangerous con man had ruined my life?

I awoke to the sound of someone knocking at the door. Looking through the peephole, I saw Jimmy standing in the rain holding bags of groceries. He came in soaked and went right into the kitchen, unloading the bags on the counter.

After a few minutes making noise in the kitchen, Jimmy came over and handed me an opened bottle of Knob Creek.

"You're watching TV with no sound?" he asked.

I looked at Jimmy, then at the bottle. I took a long swig, coughed, and put it on the coffee table, pushing Kenny's gun to the side. Not a word was traded between us as I continued to stare at the muted TV.

Jimmy lit up a cigarette and sat next to me on the couch. He picked up the bourbon and poured three fingers worth into two empty glasses.

Taking a hard drag on his cigarette, he blew out the smoke and then began nervously picking at his left thumbnails. "I spoke to Blake, the guy I told you about from the docks. He said there's a cargo ship coming in from St. Petersburg, Russia in a few days. You might be able to buy your way on it. He also gave me a phone number of a guy who does new identities. Let's take a picture of you before I leave tonight and I'll email it to him so he can get the ball rolling. I'll come back with a new passport, credit cards, social security card, and driver's license."

"How much is it all going to cost?" I asked.

"Blake said it would be around ten grand, plus or minus, and another ten for the ship's captain. That should grease enough palms to get you out safely. You'll be able to travel without anyone bothering you. That is unless you go back to your old style," Jimmy replied.

"Whose identity will I have?" I asked.

"Probably some dead guy's would be my guess."

"Better not be some wanted dead guy."

"Don't worry about it. This guy does high-quality work for the Italian Mob. He wouldn't be alive for very long if he sucked at his job," Jimmy countered.

"Yeah, I hope so because if the FBI grabs me I'll never be free again." I took another sip.

"Are you really sure they're after you?"

"I don't know. Depends how much that undercover Latino agent knows," I replied.

Jimmy stood up and pulled out his phone. It vibrated in his hand as he looked down to see who it was. He sighed and immediately answered it. "Hey. Yeah I'm leaving now. I will. Okay I'll get some on the way back."

He put the phone away, shrugged. "My old lady wants me to hurry up and stop by the store. I gotta go. Let's get that picture for your passport. Stand against that wall over there."

"Okay ready," I said.

He pulled out his phone and took some pictures. "Come on, Bill. You look like your dog just died."

Jimmy tried to make it sound like a joke, but the truth was that my heart died earlier that day.

Jimmy took a few more pictures with his phone, and looked down, thumbing through the pictures on his phone. "One of these will have to do. I gotta run,

I'll call you tomorrow and give you an update."

He finished his glass of bourbon and left. The silence in the apartment only added to my dismal mood. I sat, lit another cig, and stared again at the muted TV, then drifted deep inside my mind.

There's something about the first drag on a cig when you light it. The same rings true for the first sip of bourbon. After the first sip the flavor fades and the buzz takes over. I continued to smoke and drink like a machine trying to push the pain away. I lit cigarette after cigarette, filling the ashtray. I poured glass after glass of bourbon, watching the amber liquid ebb from the bottle. I felt filled to the brim with sorrow and hollow inside at the same time. How could I free myself of this sadness? Revenge was the only answer that had any hope of satisfaction.

A rhythmic sound filled my head, far away at first, off in the distance, slowly coming closer. The sound was very close now, right next to me. It came closer still, whispered in my ear, then sleep covered me like a warm blanket.

A dream invaded my drunken stupor. I found myself on a mountaintop high above sea level. I stepped carefully over rocks that twisted my ankles. My legs shuttered in pain with every step. Suddenly, I lost my balance and slipped down the steep incline. I tumbled down the hill, building up speed. My body spun around and I raced down on my butt like a sleigh ride, the wind blasting my face. Fear gripped me when I realized I was unable to steer or slow down, and continued my descent with increasing acceleration.

I glanced to the right and saw a huge drop. All of a sudden I crashed to a stop, now covered in deep snow. Without looking behind me to see how far I fell, I started climbing the snowy mountain in front of me. After a few steps I fell through the snow and found myself in an ice tunnel. I fought and clawed my way up through the tunnel of ice and snow surrounded me. I continued up the tube toward a bright white light at the top of the tunnel. When I reached the light I exploded out of the snow tunnel and found myself at the summit. I glazed at a glorious vista, encircled by mountain peaks and valleys. It left me feeling energized and triumphant.

I awoke sitting up. The only sound was my own breathing. The mountain top vista was etched in my mind. All I had was hope that I could escape alive, destroy my tormentors and reclaim my life. Dragging myself off the couch, I stumbled to the bedroom, exhausted, with a dry sour taste in my mouth. I flopped face down on the bed. Sleep swallowed me in its gaping maw, dark and silent.

My phone began vibrating and woke me from my drunken stupor. I went into the living room, but missed the call. It was two-thirty. Then the phone started buzzing again. I didn't recognize the number but answered out of pure stupidity.

"Yeah what do you want?"

"I want to end this game of trying to kill each other. Meet me and I'll give you back the ransom money. I want you to leave me and Dana alone," Kenny said.

"It's pretty fucking horrible when you're on the receiving end, ain't it?" I asked, smugly.

"Things just got out of hand. You know Viktor's a hot head and screwed it all up. It was never supposed to go down that way," Kenny said.

"Well it did and I guess with me in the hospital, Dana was free to date."

"You were in a fucking coma for months. I never thought you'd be coming back," he said.

"So I survived and you led me to believe that Dana was being held. Then had the Russians try to kill me for my money. C'mon man, quit with this bullshit already." I was getting irritated.

"You're right, okay? At that point everything was totally screwed up with the Russian's feud. Dmitry was still able to save your life that night. Yes, Viktor tortured you, but that just kicked off the war between them. Dmitry couldn't control Viktor or his crew. It was a blood bath, and then you had to wake up and recover, still holding a torch for Dana." I couldn't believe he was trying to justify his actions.

"I tried to talk to her. She thought I was an insane maniac and at this point that's probably what I am."

"Meet me and I'll give you the money. Let's settle this with no more shooting or games. The short time you spent with Dana is not gonna matter in the long run. She's not even interested in you anymore," Kenny said.

"Alright, I'll meet you. Just shut the fuck up already. I want double what you owe me for the time I lost. If I smell any heat, I'll shoot you before they get near me. I know all about your friend Paco and his black suited friends," I said.

"Okay where?"

"We'll meet tomorrow morning at Junior's on 44th at ten o'clock," I demanded.

"One thing Bill, I want my gun back. I like that gun."

I ended the call and wondered about this meeting. It couldn't possibly go as planned.

CHAPTER THIRTY-ONE

The next morning I woke up and went into the kitchen looking for coffee. To my dismay all I found was instant Maxwell House coffee and Earl Grey Green tea. I opted for a double scoop of instant coffee with sugar and lit a cig. Not exactly how I liked my mornings, but at least I wasn't behind bars.

At seven o'clock I called Jimmy. "Can you help me?" I asked.

I told him about my conversation with Kenny.

"You've gotta be fucking kidding, Bill. He's tricked you on every deal. How can you trust him?"

"All I can say is that it's my turn. I need you to be there this morning at nine o'clock. Check out both 44th and 45th Street. We're going to meet at Junior's on 44th at ten. I need to know if you see any FBI suits or suspicious vans before I get over there."

"Okay."

"Try not to be spotted, just keep circling.

"I'll call you once I do a few laps. Good luck and be careful."

"Thanks Jimmy," I said, and ended the call.

Next I called Patrick Sullivan. I explained what I was up to, that this could be a set-up, and that I needed his help. "Can you meet me with the payment for my recent project?"

"This is good news. Our people will handle things after you meet with Kenny. I'll be in a black limo double parked on York and 69th at eight thirty," Patrick said.

"Thank you, sir. I'll see you then."

I got dressed and headed over to meet Patrick Sullivan. I stopped at a Starbucks on Third Avenue and 66th Street. I needed a good cup of coffee. I headed over York and stood on the corner to wait for Sullivan, smoking like a chimney and sipping coffee in between drags.

After about five cigs, the black limo came around the corner, double parked, and turned on its flashing hazard lights. I walked over to the passenger side waiting to be acknowledged. I couldn't see past the black tinted windows, only my own reflection. After a while the back window rolled down, and Patrick Sullivan's face replaced my own reflection.

"You look different," he said. "I'm not sure I would have recognized you if I didn't know I was meeting you. Get in."

Patrick Sullivan studied me for a few seconds and I gave him a thin smile. "You continue to amaze me, Bill. I didn't think you'd stick around with the FBI hot on your ass. You remind me of a bulldog, with its jaws clamped down and locked on its prey. I admire your tenacity. Please take this as a goodwill gesture and a token of my appreciation," he said, and handed over manila envelope thick with what I assumed was money.

I placed the envelope on the seat to my right.

Patrick squinted, brows furrowed. His eyes darted from me to the envelope.

"Are you even gonna look?" he asked, appearing insulted.

"Oh sorry, sir. I didn't mean any disrespect."

"I hope it helps you settle the loose ends you've

mentioned. You'll still have a job waiting for you in our organization when you are finished," Patrick said, with a slight nod.

I opened the envelope and found six bundles of hundred dollar bills wrapped with rubber bands. Surprised by the large amount, I smiled. "Thank you, sir. This is a very generous."

Patrick tilted his head to the side and cracked his neck. "I want you to know that because of your quick thinking Morgan is going to recover from his injuries."

"It was my cousin Jimmy that got us both to the hospital. Jimmy stepped up to save us."

"I had heard he was a drug addict. That's very surprising," Patrick said.

"Jimmy's been clean for almost a year. He recently got married. He's come a long way and can be counted on. If it wasn't for him, Morgan might be dead." "I didn't realize he'd played such a big part."

"Can I ask you a favor? Can you let Jimmy continue working with your crew?"

"I'll see what I can do," said Patrick. "You go ahead, have your meeting, and we'll catch up with Kenny at some point. I expect that the FBI will keep us at bay for a while. Either way we will track him. It may be difficult, but we'll take care of that rat. I wish you good luck. Contact me again when you're ready to work."

I left Patrick Sullivan and on my way to meet Kenny my phone went off. It was Jimmy. "How's it looking?"

"There's definitely some activity," he said. "I saw a couple of vans with dark tinted windows and groups of wise guys standing around in blazers. It looks like everyone's waiting for a special guest to get here," Jimmy said.

"This may be harder than I thought," I said, letting out a big sigh.

"What… Whatcha gonna do?" Jimmy asked, with a nervous stammer.

"Wait, I have an idea. You're going to meet with Kenny…"

Jimmy cut me off. "Hold it. I'm already in too deep," Jimmy said.

"Just hear me out, and I'll handle the whole thing. I need you to just go into the restaurant, sit at his table, and order raspberry cheesecake. Don't sit down until you see him at a table waiting. I'll be right behind you, ready to do the rest," I said.

"Okay, let's do this," he said, trying to be brave.

"Alright brother."

At nine fifty-five Kenny entered Junior's carrying a gym bag and was seated. I arrived in time to see Jimmy enter and sit at Kenny's table. I asked to be seated on the other side of the restaurant and left my black leather jacket hanging over the chair. I knew my white shirt and black pants made me look like a waiter, and I quickly grabbed a pad, pen, and towel from the waiter's station and went over to take their order. They had already started talking when I stepped over to their table.

"Would you like some coffee to start?" I asked.

Jimmy right on queue said, "I'll have a slice of raspberry cheesecake and a regular coffee."

"I'll just have coffee," Kenny said, trailing off as he recognized me.

I had Kenny's gun in my hand under the towel. "Make any abrupt moves and you'll regret it. Now give Jimmy the gym bag so he can see the two hundred thousand." Kenny slowly handed the bag to Jimmy. He unzipped it only enough to see some of the money and feel around for the rest. He looked up and nodded. A wide grin crossed his face.

"Here you go, brother," Jimmy said. He zipped up the bag and handed it to me.

"As promised, here's your favorite gun," I said, and placed it on the table under the towel.

"You're not gonna make it outta here," Kenny said, feeling confident and putting his hand under the towel.

"You said no more tricks."

"I lied," he said, pulling out the gun.

"HE'S GOT A GUN!" I yelled.

Before Kenny had a chance to react, I swung the bag full force. It hit him straight in the face, knocking him and the chair over. The last thing I saw as I grabbed my black leather jacket and pushed Jimmy out of the restaurant was Kenny's feet in the air. On the way out, I heard crashing tables and people yelling.

Kenny struggled to get up, waving the gun around in front of him. People in the restaurant screamed and dove away from the man with the gun. He pointed the gun at me and squeezed the trigger several times, but it was empty. An off-duty police officer tackled Kenny and started pounding him with his fists. A second later Kenny was in handcuffs as a stampede of customers followed us out of the restaurant and into the street. To add to the confusion, black-suited FBI agents came running into the restaurant.

We rushed over to Eighth Avenue and caught a taxi uptown to 57th Street, then walked over to Ninth Avenue and took another taxi to Tracy's apartment. Once inside, Jimmy pulled out the bourbon and poured a nice amount in each glass. He held up his glass for a toast. "Here's to a job well done. Now go get that fucking asshole, Viktor," he said.

We brought our glasses together, with a clink. "And here's to you, brother. I couldn't have done it without you," I said, letting out a slight cough and clinking Jimmy's glass again.

CHAPTER THIRTY-TWO

Jimmy called Tracy that night to let her know that everything was fine. He told her that I needed his help and was staying over at the apartment. We drank the rest of the Knob Creek, and filled up a large ashtray with cigarette butts. I went to bed completely exhausted. Jimmy stayed up to watch TV. I heard him laughing at something before I passed out in the bedroom.

The next morning I got up early. I made a couple of mugs of coffee and sat down on the couch next to Jimmy, who was snoring loudly. I turned on the TV, lit up a cig, sipped the coffee and watched the news. Not a word about a gunman being arrested at Junior's.

I grabbed my black leather jacket, which hung over the kitchen chair and took out Patrick's money from the inside pockets. I placed six stacks of hundred dollar bills on the coffee table. Each stack was ten thousand dollars. I picked up the gym bag and emptied it out next to the stacks, two hundred sixty thousand dollars. I slapped Jimmy on the leg. "Do you believe all this shit is real?"

Jimmy jumped up and held up his hands. "I didn't fucking do anything," he blurted out, trying to get an idea where he was.

He squinted his eyes and looked at the pile of cash. "Whoa! That's a shit load of cash, brother."

"And some of it's yours," I said.

"What are you talking about?"

I counted out ten stacks. "Here's the wedding present I couldn't give while I was in a coma," I said.

Jimmy just sat there, blinking at the money. I patted his back. "Kenny owes me a lot more for ruining my life, but I wanna share some of his money with you and Tracy."

"Wow, Bill. I don't know what to say. I've never had that much money before." Tears filled his eyes.

"Why are you crying?" I asked.

"Cause it's so fucking beautiful," he said, wiping

his face with a shirtsleeve.

"I owe you and Tracy for sticking out your necks. Once I'm back from my vacation maybe things will get better for me too," I said, feeling a little unsure.

"Let me go check on the identity stuff and the ship arrangements. I'll give you a buzz later. Everything should be done today and we can get you on your way," Jimmy said, trying to give me some hope.

"Be careful. I'm not sure how safe it is for you," I said.

"I doubt he's interested in me. I didn't do anything to him and the FBI isn't after me," Jimmy said.

"Don't be stupid. How do you know? They might try to follow you to get to me. Just make sure you're not being followed. Stay away from your place until I'm on my way."

"Tracy will never go for that. One night is okay, but a few and I'll be in the doghouse. I'll move things along and be back in a few hours," Jimmy said.

Then he bolted up, went into the kitchen, and came out with a small shopping bag. He scooped up the money, put it in the bag, and rushed out, slamming the door behind him.

I opened the gym bag, placed it on the floor at the edge of the table, and slowly dragged my forearm across the table. The stacks of hundred cascaded over the edge, tumbling like a waterfall into the waiting fissure. There had to be a way for me to put the money someplace safe and still withdraw cash as needed overseas.

Later that afternoon Jimmy called.

"I picked up your papers, but there's a change with the ship," he told me. "It was supposed to come into New York but is now going to dock in Newark, New Jersey. We can head over there tomorrow, pay off the captain, and get you on board."

"I need to set up a bank account to access my money from Europe or Russia."

"I'll be over in an hour or so. Just hang tight."

"Remember to make sure you aren't followed."

"I will. Things look cool so far. Don't be so paranoid," he said, and ended the call.

Jimmy ran late, and I started pacing in the apartment. The day was slipping away. My cigarettes were running low so I did sets of pushups and crunches to reduce my anxiety. At around four o'clock

Jimmy showed up with a carton of Marlboro Reds and another bottle of Knob Creek, plus some food.

"Sorry I'm late Bill, I was trying to make sure everything is clear. I grabbed a few things at the deli a few blocks away, but they didn't have much," Jimmy said, a little nervous. He handed me a large envelope. "Here, look this over and make sure you're happy with everything. I glanced at it and it looked pretty fucking professional."

I opened the envelope and dumped the contents onto the coffee table. A passport, two credit cards, social security card, and driver's license. I opened the passport. John Wilfred O'Brien. "It feels a little funny to have a new name. Maybe I'll get used to it after a while."

"Maybe."

"It all looks official to me, but I'm no expert."

"I guess if it passes at the bank tomorrow, then you'll know it's good enough," Jimmy said.

"I'll give it a shot."

"I'll know more tomorrow about the ship's port and departure. We're close, so just hang in there and be careful walking around town."

"You gonna stay a while and have a couple of drinks?"

"Nah, I gotta go. I'm having dinner with Tracy."

"Okay, enjoy, and tell her thanks for everything."

"I will. See ya tomorrow. I'll call you as soon as I hear something," he said as he left.

The next morning I awoke ready to get to the bank and test out my new identity. If there were any problems I'd need to know it now. I took a scalding shower, shaved, brushed my teeth and skipped the instant coffee.

I left the apartment and headed to the bank. I sat for a while in a chair next to an old woman who needed help cashing in her coins. Once she was attended to, a blond librarian type in a business suit came over.

"Can I help you, sir? I'm assistant manager Jenna Johnson." She gave me a big smile with the whitest teeth I'd ever seen.

"Yes, I would like to open a new account," I said.

"Absolutely, please come right this way. Have a seat Mister...?" She said, and straightened her skirt before taking a seat behind a polished wood desk.

"Bill... I mean John Wilfred O'Brien. I use my middle name. Bill is fine," I said, putting the gym bag on my lap. When I handed over the hundred thousand dollars in cash, her hands shook, and she seemed a little nervous as she filled out the last of the paperwork.

I wondered what she looked like once her glasses and clothes were off, her hair hanging down, without the frumpy corporate look. I explained that I was traveling overseas for a few months and needed access. I suddenly felt very sad and lonely.

My license and passport worked great without a hitch. After a few signatures we shook hands, and I was on my way.

Jimmy called on my way back to Tracy's. "Hey Jimmy."

"Good news," he said. "The ship's name is *Eibek* and is docked at Port Newark in New Jersey. We meet the captain, Igor Kozlov, tomorrow at four in the morning. You can give him your donation and join his crew for the trip," Jimmy explained. "I'll get a taxi and pick you up at around three." I hung up the phone and thought about the trip over the Atlantic to a country I didn't know. I had no way of anticipating what I would face on my journey or how I was going to get Viktor.

CHAPTER THIRTY-THREE

Jimmy arrived at about three fifteen. On the way through the Holland Tunnel into New Jersey, Jimmy enlightened me about the captain. "Just try to hang back and say as little as possible to him. My friend told me he has a reputation for being very gruff. Hopefully he'll be happy with your donation."

After thirty-five minutes we arrived at the Marine Terminal. The taxi driver drove down E. Port Street, which ended at a security checkpoint.

We got out and Jimmy paid him. "There'll be a few extra twenties if you wait to take me back," Jimmy told him. Keep the meter running."

We walked over to the security booth and spoke to the guards. "We're meeting with Captain Kozlov of the *Eilbek*," Jimmy told them.

The guard checked for our names on his clipboard. He flipped through a few pages and nodded letting us through.

As we passed security I noticed the first ship docked at the pier. The ship's size was impressive, longer than a football field, and it made me feel small in comparison. Bright floodlights lit up the activities on the docks as workers rushed around, loading supplies and preparing for departure. It was hard to believe that it was only four in the morning.

We walked down to the second ship. *Eilbek* was painted in white text on the side of a giant black ship with a red bottom. A large crane loaded a blue forty-foot long metal container onto the ship's deck. The sound of the containers being stacked was deafening. I watched in awe as the crane picked up a blue container that weighed tons and placed it on the deck with a loud boom, before it went back for another container.

We found the captain further down on the dock yelling in Russian at the dockworkers. He seemed oblivious to our presence. A clean-shaven, short man with a stone face and a wide stocky frame, he wore a navy cap with a navy wool coat and black rubber boots.

He turned to greet us, and sneered in a heavy Russian accent, "What in the fuck do you want?"

"I'm Jimmy Campbell and this is John O'Brien," Jimmy said.

"Yeah, so who cares? I have no time for dis bullshit," he blurted, turned and walked away.

"We were told to be here at four this morning, and that for the right donation, you might let my friend come aboard and travel to your next port. Is that still the case?" Jimmy inquired.

"Oh yeah, now I remember. He wants to leave America? Da?" the Captain said, slightly changing his disposition.

"Yes, that's right," Jimmy said.

"So what are you waiting for?" he asked.

Jimmy handed the captain the ten thousand dollars that I had given him earlier in the week. He looked into the envelope and nodded.

"This will do," he said.

I reached between them and handed the captain another ten thousand. "Is there any way to keep me in separate quarters?" I asked.

"This is very good. Are you some kind of big

shot? Da, something can be arranged. My assistant is not on vessel. You can use his quarters until we pick him up at Port of Rotterdam," he said, a thin crooked smile crossing his face. He pointed towards the ship. "You go up da ramp and wait for me. We leave in two hours."

The captain went back to yelling commands at the dockworkers, then turned and started up the ramp.

I gave Jimmy a big hug. "Thanks, brother. I'll see you in a few weeks."

I didn't know how long I'd be gone for, a few weeks, a few months, or if I was even going to make it back alive. I was proud of Jimmy for how he had turned his life around and had truly become like a real brother to me. I would miss him and I was worried for his safety while I was gone.

"Good luck, Bill, and be safe," he said, and walked off deep in thought.

I followed the Captain up the narrow ramp, carrying my two bags. When we got onto the deck of the ship he barked at the crew in Russian. They nodded and cleared out, rushing off to take care of his request.

"You come with me," he said.

Holding onto the railing, I followed him along the edge of the deck and through a narrow doorway. We climbed the stairs to the fourth level. It was dark, lit only by dull lights at the top of each landing. Once we reached the landing, he opened the door, and we entered the control room. He walked in, reached under a small table covered with maps, and pulled out a bottle of vodka and two small shot glasses.

"Now we drink," he said, pouring vodka into the glasses and handing one to me.

He knocked back the clear liquid and eyed me. I drank the vodka and he immediately refilled my glass.

"We have a long trip so relax. You'll pay again to come back? Right my friend?"

"Well, if I have a good trip." I said, smiling.

He looked down at my two large bags, then looked behind me and sighed. Stepping over to an intercom he started yelling in Russian at one of his crew who was somewhere on the ship. He wiped his brow with a rag.

"I apologize for da delay. I had to clear somebody out of da cabin. Here is a key to lock your things. Now we drink? It is good, very good, da?" he said, clinking his glass against mine.

"When do we leave, captain?" I asked, drinking my shot.

"Call me Igor, my new friend. We leave as soon as these fookin asses finish loading containers," he said and poured another shot. He looked at me to see if I was still drinking with him.

I nodded and he filled my shot glass. One of the crew came in and spoke to the captain in Russian. He seemed pleased and turned to me. "Everything is ready for you, John. Let's go."

I picked up my bags and followed Igor down to the third level, and then into a small door that led to a narrow hallway. An echo rang out as our feet clanked on the metal floor. We walked down the hallway passing many doors of other crewmembers.

We finally arrived at my cabin. I stepped into the small room, which had a single bed, a locker and a small narrow table with a lamp.

"So? Is this great or what?"

"This will do fine," I replied.

"Dis is very good. Come out on deck in an hour and we will be pulled out into the harbor," he said. As he headed out, he looked very satisfied with himself. "Remember come out in one hour. You'll want to see the view as we leave your country," he said, and closed the door.

I put my bags in the locker and locked it with a padlock that was hanging there with a key inserted. I felt a little funny about leaving my weapons in the locker, but I took a handgun and a knife from the bag. I sat on the edge of the bed and rubbed my face, tired and trying to prepare myself for the long trip.

I pulled out a paperback novel and started reading. The novel was *Shantaram* by Gregory David Roberts. It's the story of a guy who escapes from prison in Australia to hide in India. I was reading in the small bed, when I felt the ship move and realized it was time to go up on the deck.

CHAPTER THIRTY-FOUR

I descended the stairs to the deck of the ship and found several crewmembers leaning over the railing. Looking out as we pulled away from the Port of Newark, I didn't know how long it would be before I saw land again. The sky was grey with low-hanging clouds and a cold wind blowing from the east. I cupped my hands around my lighter and lit my cigarette. I took the smoke deep into my lungs, then slowly exhaled.

I stared at the dock as we navigated out into the harbor. We passed lower Manhattan, then Brooklyn, then the edge of Long Island, and then out into the Atlantic Ocean.

The salty aroma of the sea surrounded me. A spray of ocean mist landed on my face as the ship gained speed in the open water. I watched, as my hometown grew smaller in the distance. A city so beautiful, so full of opportunity and success for some people, but for me it held only pain and sadness.

The clouds and the ocean seemed to merge on the horizon, with the same grey pallor. The air was cold and the ocean mist only added to the grey dismal mood. I wasn't sure what I was going to find on the other side of the world, but I knew it wasn't going to beat me. Viktor had to die, and nothing would stand in my way.

I took a hard drag on my cigarette and flicked it into the grey water. The red trail disappeared into the waves below. A chill went up my spine. I turned up the collar of my black leather jacket and put my hands in the pockets.

As I walked around the deck, cliques of men huddled together talking and smoking. Much like the gangs and crews of New York, they clung to each other due to affiliations or nationality. One group was making a lot of noise, laughing and creating a ruckus. Two of the crewmembers wrestled, play fighting and amusing the others. One guy fell over onto the floor and howled with laughter. I noticed a handgun sticking out of his waistband and knew I wasn't the only one carrying weapons on board.

As I climbed the narrow metal stairs to my cabin in the ship's tower, a cloud of sadness and regret hovered over me. Fatigue and exhaustion took my last bit of energy; I sighed and closed the cabin door.

I collapsed into bed and stared at the metal riveted ceiling. I could feel the ship rise and fall against the waves, a gentle swaying in the open ocean. The sound of my own breathing filled my ears. My eyes became heavy and the darkness swallowed me in its black silence.

ABOUT THE AUTHOR

Garrard Hayes is a lifelong New York resident whose ancestors made their living on the streets of Manhattan and Brooklyn. His love of action and crime fiction, together with a knack for good, gritty story telling, sparked him to write. He lives in New York with his wife, two children, and three dogs.